Hostage in Illyria

HOSTAGE IN ILLYRIA
A Novel of Suspense

CONSTANCE LEONARD

DODD, MEAD & COMPANY · NEW YORK

LIBRARY OF CONGRESS CATALOGING IN PUBLICATION DATA

Leonard, Constance.
    Hostage in Illyria.

    I. Title
PZ4.L5797Ho [PS3562.E54] 813'.5'4 76–7979
ISBN 0–396–07323–9

For Jill

Hostage in Illyria

Chapter 1

There were probably several factors in her ultimate decision—if it was a decision; she had not made a decision for a long time, not been able to—so that it was not as hasty, not as rash as it seemed.

The tinted glass in the fat air-conditioned tour bus was only one of them, the underwater feeling it gave her of being a fish in a giant aquarium, swimming, sloshing all the way from Zagreb to the Dalmatian coast. A certain squashiness about the motion of the bus reinforced this woozy feeling as they swayed around curves down the plunging road.

Assorted squeals issued from the seats behind her, a terrible jollity: this after all was the thrill they had paid for, like roller coaster riders. The blue-haired widows were the best of sports, a bridge foursome, all in drip-dry pant suits of pretty colors. Marianna disliked herself for being churlish. They had meant to be kind, counting her as one of them, although younger, of course—her hair was brown still and swung free—and she was not needed for bridge.

"Mrs. Eames . . . Marianna?" Mr. Whitcomb, whom she refused to call Allen, touched her wrist. He was always touching her, always next to her and touching her in subtle little ways that were to pass for accidents. He should have known better at his age. Sixty at least —yes, he said that he had retired from General Motors —he was clearly hipped on romance. And I suppose I look young to him, Marianna thought, startled, being half his age; she had not felt young, not for a long time. His wife had been dead for several years. Are we a whole busload of relics then? She was being extreme. In fact there were several middle-aged couples, the restaurant owners from Bethesda and the Howard professor and his wife, and a homosexual pair—one of them theatrically handsome from a distance—and two honeymooners. And the college dropout with his arthritic mother. And . . .

Mr. Whitcomb's hand closed over hers now and squeezed. "You're very quiet, Marianna. Are you all right?"

"I'm fine, just fine." She snatched back her hand and sat as far away from him as she could, pressed against the window. And who am I to be rude, she thought angrily; not angry with him but with herself. She should have felt sorry for him at least, sympathetic. Weren't they two of a kind in a way, both in desperate need of a miracle?

It had been a year and a half, almost exactly eighteen months without Ted. She rested her forehead against the glass and closed her eyes, shutting out the plum-

2

meting curves and the distant blue, hazy promise of the Adriatic.

The shoal of their luggage massed around the elevators in the lobby was another thing, and the bellboy's expressive eyebrows, his *mon Dieu* look, or whatever the Serbian equivalent was. Too many suitcases, a god-awful vulgar excess, and too many people, a great unwieldy herd of us milling about in noisy confusion, clueless without our leader. Whatever merit we may have individually, Marianna decided, does not shine through in these circumstances; *en masse,* we are unattractive. She could not help noticing the dismay in the attitudes of the other hotel guests, how they kept their distance. She would have walked away, too, disassociated herself.

"My dear, your key! Room 419, you and Miss Hawthorne." Ivo was triumphant, flourishing the key over his head as if it were no mean achievement, in a class with a slain dragon. He was young for a tour leader, shiny-eyed and earnest. "My dear" was a beguiling souvenir of his year in Britain.

"Lucky Miss Hawthorne," Mr. Whitcomb murmured and laughed, excited by his daring. In the crush he had managed to be next to Marianna again, to rub up against her.

She thought of several rude and childish retorts. She could spit in his eye, she was tall enough. Instead she reached for the key. "Thanks. Come on, Miss Hawthorne. I guess we're all set. Shall we try for the elevator?"

"You must call me Anita . . . if we're to be roomies!" Miss Hawthorne's enthusiasm never faltered. She was admissions lady at a girls' boarding school, and Marianna imagined that she had been a student there, too, in those very same mock-Tudor halls and had simply stayed on, slowly drying and graying through the years but with her undergraduate spirit intact.

The matter of double occupancy had been in the small print—and an economy—and would have to be seen to, Marianna realized. Miss Hawthorne was no more acceptable than Mr. Whitcomb. She was too used to being alone. But her protest was silent, limp, and she stood patiently waiting for the elevator. The decision had been made for her . . . as all the arrangements had and would be, tour without end, wasn't that the point?

The blackboard next to the elevator said it all: when, to the precise minute, she was to be thirsty, hungry, sleepy, or up and dressed, bright-eyed and bushy-tailed, on deck for city tour of Split at 0900 hours, bus to Trogir at 1500 hours, gambling at 2100 hours. Good God—without warning Ted's voice came alive, a hoot of laughter and some raunchy revisions in the schedule. Marianna let herself be jostled into the elevator and carried on up, wherever they said.

At dinner the tour group was bunched at one end of the long dining room, the kitchen end which, undoubtedly more convenient for the waiters, was farthest from the view of the harbor. Their own menu, in English, obviated difficult choices. "Oh, lovely," Miss Haw-

4

thorne said, "don't you agree?" And it was hard to guess whether she meant the egg bobbing in her soup or the whole starchy room, the formally coated waiters and stiff little bunches of orange calendulas on the tables.

There was one elderly waiter and a platoon of young ones, learning, already adept at dealing out plates and apportioning meat, spooning out sauce with a snappy flourish. Marianna sipped her wine and moved her knees away from Mr. Whitcomb's. He poked at his pale meat, blank-faced.

"Veal," said Miss Hawthorne. "The Italian influence, of course! Since they're virtually neighbors across the Adriatic. Perhaps not quite so tasty as the Roman, still . . ." She dabbed at the corners of her mouth. She was not used to wine; nor, it became evident as the meal progressed, were the bridge ladies, all in their floral gowns after, Marianna imagined, due consultation. Their voices shrilled through the room, turning heads. Marianna could feel the stares, the amusement, the condescension.

A peak of hilarity was reached with the opening of the Casino, a giggly sort of deviltry which, starting tentatively in the anteroom in front of a bank of slot machines, crescendoed at the roulette table. Marianna ordered Turkish coffee at the bar, her back to them all.

"They're having fun anyway," the man next to her said. "Don't knock it. And the Casino needs business." He ordered *vinjak* and swung sideways on the barstool, facing her.

She had seen him before in the dining room, at the

far end by the open windows, noticed the shape of his head against the evening light.

"American?"

"You can't tell?" She laughed and looked at him. Thick, springy red-brown hair and sideburns, grizzled at the edges, made his head look big. His chin was definite, rather long; deep radial lines around his eyes showed paler than his sunburn.

"I meant you," he said. "There's no doubt about them. It's all right, could be worse." He was laughing at her. "I'm one myself. Paul Currier."

She found herself shaking hands, unsure of herself. She was not used to picking up strangers in bars, and this one, this Paul Currier, seemed to be entertained by her hesitance. He continued to smile, watching her closely as if he could see through her and knew that he could break down her reserve . . . as if they were practically friends already, and this was a private party. Or a private joke.

"Marianna Eames," she said.

He glanced at her hands. "Mrs."

"Yes." She was abrupt. She had not meant to explain, but she heard herself go on, her stomach clutching. "I'm a widow."

"I'm sorry." He did not dwell on the fact. "East coast?"

"Yes."

"Okay, I've got all night. All week, all month, if necessary. I can extract one small fact at a time, like teeth, or we can talk, like people, no language problem." He folded his arms.

"I'm from Washington. D.C.," she added. "There, that's two teeth at once. Georgetown, for another. How's that for garrulous?"

"No kidding. We're practically neighbors. Well, near enough. *Dobro došli.*"

"What on earth does that mean?"

"Welcome."

It was easy then—and absurd, the pleasure of this silly game of do-you-know? and the odd comfort she felt in talking about home. Ridiculous to have come all this way to talk about the very place she most needed to leave, to be sitting here in this cavernous new hotel in Yugoslavia with a man she had known for barely five minutes, in spirit walking with him up and down the cobbled, miniature streets of Georgetown. He did not seem like a stranger. He knew the tiny decorating shop that she and Margot had—or said that he did.

"On Wisconsin Avenue, right?"

"Just above P. Known as p's & q's, naturally, lower case. I'm afraid we were in a cutesy mood, but we had some lovely things and a lot of fun handing out good advice. We were terribly sure of ourselves, young . . ."

That was how it had been, how she had been before —good at things, confident, decisive—before it happened, before this last year, the past eighteen months.

He waited, puzzled, but not pressuring her, as if he

could see her vitality draining away, like sawdust. In the long silence he ordered *vinjak* again, two this time, without consulting her.

" 'And now I am six, I'm as clever as clever,' " he murmured at last, so softly that she did not have to hear him. She did hear him, gratefully, and smiled.

He raised his glass. "*Živeli!* Which means exactly what you think it means. You'll find I'm a confirmed showoff and will soon have shown off my entire vocabulary, Serbo and/or Croatian. Now . . ."

"Your turn," she said.

He rattled off the facts of his life as if he were filling out a form, fitting the answers into small spaces. Born Connecticut, educated Columbia, ten years Foreign Service, seven years teaching history at American University, which brought him up to his current devoutly-to-be-indulged-in sabbatical. "My theory being," he expanded, "that a decade or so is enough of just about anything. Time for a change. Anyway, I'd always wanted to try teaching and my older brother is in Foreign Service, going great guns. I figured one of us was enough."

He paused and Marianna sensed, *knew* that he was coming to his wife. She had an odd sensation of bracing herself. He went on then as he had before, his tone light and factual. "My marriage, by the way, lasted twelve years, a case in point. My wife chose to stick with the diplomatic—a First Secretary to be exact—and at last report was maintaining a high standard of living in Brasilia, the perks of a professor being nothing to compare."

It was Marianna who said "I'm sorry," this time, the conventional response.

He shrugged and touched her glass. "Another of those for strength, before we join the ladies? I'm prepared to blow a few dinars at roulette."

She shook her head.

"You're sure?" he said as shrieks of victory emanated from the Casino. He tipped up his glass then and put money on the bar. Smiling, he asked one more question. "Just how did you get mixed up with that bunch of rowdies?"

How did she? Not rationally, certainly not by weighing the pros and cons and coming to an intelligent decision. That was the point, wasn't it, that she was incapable of anything of the sort? She tried, not altogether successfully, to match his tone. "Actually, I think it was Margot's doing . . . to get me out of the shop, anywhere, away. I was no help to her, to anyone, the way I was. A liability rather, depressing everyone. I was a zombie."

He was unconvinced, frowning at her, and somehow it became important to make him understand. "The idea, I guess, was to push me into something entirely different, new to me, places where Ted and I had never been. But in safe custody, with someone to shepherd me around and see that I got on and off the right planes or whatever and ate my meals—to cope with everything, since I couldn't. Left to my own devices, I'd still be in Washington at the travel agency, paralyzed by indecision."

"All this," he said—he was wonderfully gentle—"after your husband died?"

"After I killed him," she said.

Shrill women's voices filled the silence, and the metallic spill of a slot machine paying off. He waited, his expression neutral. When she did at last go on, it was in a deadened voice, so that he had to lean forward and watch her lips closely to be sure what she was saying— to be sure sometimes that she was saying anything at all; there were long pauses.

"I was driving. I hit a slick place . . . oil, ice, I don't know . . . it was a dreadful night. There was a car coming the other way . . . a lot of cars, on the expressway . . . the end of the holiday weekend. We spun around somehow. I've never been quite sure what happened. I've gone over and over it. They think Ted's door must have sprung open. He was thrown out . . . in front of another car."

"Oh, Lord." He made a move to touch her, then drew back his hand. "But it wasn't your fault."

She stared at him a little wildly. "You don't understand. We had no business being there at all . . . on that road, that night. It was all my idea. I insisted. Ted wanted to wait until morning. When it started to snow, he said there'd be too many fool drivers on the roads, driving too fast for the conditions. You know how it is, they're not used to snow around there and this was the first . . ."

She paused longer than usual. "As if he *knew* . . . some sort of premonition. I don't know . . ."

She rubbed her forehead as if she could erase this thought, then became almost brisk, factual, repeating words that she had said before, often. "We'd been to Philadelphia—Jenkintown—for Thanksgiving with my parents. We'd been there the whole long weekend and I was itchy to get home. It was the shop really. I had an appointment with a new client early Monday morning. It seemed terribly important. I was full of myself in those days, my clients, my career . . . dear God, you'd have thought the fate of the nation was involved."

He smiled. "Happens to people in Washington."

He *was* listening—not only listening, but hearing what she was trying to say, understanding. The knowledge gave her peculiar comfort, a kind of easing; without touching her, he had unsnarled the hard tangle of nerves at the back of her neck. But he did not mean to interrupt her, he made that clear as well.

"Ted had appointments, too. Important clients. His probably were important. He was with Kennett and Kahn, the lawyers. But he wasn't all that impressed. He said they could wait if necessary, we could start back early in the morning if the snow stopped." She faltered on that. "God knows what I was trying to prove. It was all so senseless. So stubborn. We had a colossal row. I suppose my parents sided with him and I thought they were being too cautious for words, too protective—

they always could get my back up. Anyway . . .

"I decided that I had to go back and I packed myself into the car. I told Ted he didn't have to come. He could stay if he wanted to . . .

"Don't say anything, please . . ."

He handed her a small paper napkin as her tears welled, then another. She got hold of herself almost immediately, blotted her face, blew her nose and apologized with a slight crack in her voice. "Sympathy always undoes me," she said.

"Funny how easy it is to talk to strangers," he said quietly, and the obverse was there, clearly, between them.

Neither of them needed to say any more. For several minutes they followed their own thoughts in a comfortable silence which might have gone on much longer if Miss Hawthorne had not materialized.

"There you are, roomy! I wondered. I thought you'd pooped out on us. But you're not gambling," she noted, and Marianna sensed disapproval, as if she had let down the team by cutting gym class. Perhaps she imagined that, out of guilt, and Miss Hawthorne's reaction when Paul turned and stood up and she realized that he was not one of their group: the loaded little wide-eyed "Oh!"

"Well!" she said when Marianna had completed introductions. "I know that I for one am off to bed; it's way past my bedtime! And we all need our beauty sleep, don't we, and plenty of rest, goodness knows, to keep up the pace. Sightseeing early tomorrow. Diocletian's Palace! Are you coming, roomy? Shall we go up together?"

Marianna found that she had slipped off the bar chair, ready to follow along. Paul did not urge her to stay. He, too, seemed to accept Miss Hawthorne's decision. He put out his hand exactly as he had to Miss Hawthorne when they were introduced and said, "Good night."

Chapter 2

"The great Roman Emperor Diocletian," Ivo said grandly, "was born very near here, and when toward the end of his life he relinquished his power and returned home to live out his days in tranquillity, he caused this superb palace to be built . . ."

"Local boy makes good!" Mr. Whitcomb said in her ear so that Marianna missed whatever Ivo said next.

". . . fourth century, as both a summer residence and a fortress," Ivo earnestly recited.

"Wow!" said Mr. Whitcomb with a nudge. "They don't build 'em like they used to."

Marianna walked away. The massive stone walls with their high-arched windows and columns rose white against a brilliant blue sky. The wispiest of clouds were being hustled past. The palace itself in its scope and complexity was incomprehensible at first, more of a walled town—and a bustling one where people lived and worked and did their marketing, even their laundry, and strung their sheets like white pennants on the battlements. It was, Marianna thought, a little as if peo-

14

ple hung their wash out to dry between the classic columns of the Lincoln Memorial, or opened up shops between the pillars at Mount Vernon.

The push of ordinary modern life disrupted the tour group, separating them, so that Ivo's voice became a conscientious drone, the words indistinguishable. Marianna had an impulse to lag behind. She wanted to run her hand along the rough stone wall, to absorb it somehow, the ancient strength of it, and to establish her own relationship with this sunlit interior square. She could see Ivo's raised arm pointing and the familiar heads bobbing after him, Miss Hawthorne's eagerly elongated neck and the widows' hair, lavender in this light.

She let them go by default. She was ready for a brief flicker of panic and could manage it. She could not possibly get lost. The palace faced the harbor as the hotel did, an easy walk away along a sidewalk that followed the curve of the shore. She let herself drift, moved by the prevailing motion of the crowd as they did their everyday errands or took their coffee breaks in the venerable courtyards and shop-lined arcades. Unable to speak to them or understand what they were saying, she felt anonymous and invisible, a little like a ghost floating across the worn paving stones. There was a flower stall by one great square gateway and a table of tiny vials, lavender oil and rosemary, she recognized, sniffing. She did not try to buy anything; the simplest transaction seemed too difficult, even a cup of coffee beyond her capabilities. She would have liked coffee and to sit at one of the little tables where bright umbrellas were blossoming now like giant flowers opening in the sun.

To sit with someone: loneliness hit her then. She was not frightened yet, but sharply aware like a swimmer who finds that she has gone a little too far beyond her depth when there is no one to hear her call for help.

She had not seen Paul Currier that morning. He was not in the breakfast room, nor the lobby, and it occurred to her now that he might not be staying at the hotel at all. He had not said that he was. For all his apparent candor, in fact, he had told her very little about himself *now,* his present and future plans. He had been a good listener instead.

She found her way out of the palace, back to the open, windy palm-lined street. There were motley fishing boats, a faint smell of tar, and giant civic flower beds, gaudy with purple and yellow pansies and red geraniums. She had not expected such a wealth of flowers, the fat bushes of daisies and heavily fragrant hedges everywhere. What had she expected . . . a lifeless monotone, a subjective grayness?

Paul was in the solarium beyond the dining room, stretched out on a long chair beside the pool. There was a somber-looking book propped on his stomach, a pile of others on the tile floor beside him. He slid dark glasses down his nose and peered up at her.

"Hi."

"Hi." She felt an enormous relief, all out of proportion in the circumstances, as if she had made it back to

16

shore. He kept a finger in his book to mark his place and apologized in a preoccupied murmur for not getting up.

"I won't interrupt. I'm on my way to lunch anyway," she said.

"Enjoy the sights? I gather you're getting the full treatment. Trogir this afternoon *and* Kastella? Heroic, I call it, and a damn sight more than most of us can handle; too many centuries for one day." He smiled a little sadly. "All of ancient Illyria. Greeks, Romans, Byzantines . . . the whole Renaissance at a gulp. Maybe I'm getting old."

He stretched as he said this and moved to make room for her on the chaise beside him. "Why not slow down? Come swim with me this afternoon. To hell with Trogir."

"But I've got to see everything, it's what I came for." Her refusal was automatic, a reflex. Everything had already been planned for her, part of the package.

"And paid for? You're right, you want to get your money's worth. Okay, I'll tell you what. Swim this afternoon and I'll take you to Trogir tomorrow myself, a personally conducted tour. Without undue modesty, I think I could match spiels with Ivo any day."

"But I won't be here. We're leaving tomorrow."

"The bus is," he said. "You don't have to, you know."

It was not so much a decision as inertia, another default, Marianna reasoned, that kept her from the Trogir tour. She was still not committed to anything, at least

17

anything beyond this one truant afternoon. Her excuses, moreover, were more than half true. She was a little tired, she had been walking all morning, and if her tireless roommate found such weakness inexcusable, *tant pis!* Why in any case did she feel it necessary to explain? The ladies could and undoubtedly would draw their own conclusions.

Meanwhile there was the afternoon: motionless, sheltered, under glass. An unnatural greenhouse light filled the solarium, and a taint of chlorine. Alone, so that every sound was exaggerated in the echoing space, they talked softly and for long intervals not at all, at ease with each other like old friends—or a married couple. Marianna leafed through a guidebook for a while, then closed her eyes.

"Makarska . . . Ploče . . . Dubrovnik. Is that your route?"

She was jolted awake, feeling lost and unguarded for an instant.

"Sorry. I didn't know you were asleep."

"Neither did I." Her heart gradually stopped hammering. To clear her head she slipped into the pool and swam across it, then back again and held onto the edge at Paul's feet.

"How's the water?"

"Bliss," she said.

"You don't feel underprivileged then, cheated out of Trogir?"

They smiled at each other. She pulled off her bathing

cap and shook out her hair, then climbed out of the pool and stood dripping into puddles.

"It's a perfectly good route," Paul said, returning to his subject. "Spectacular, in fact . . . this whole coast is, whichever way you go at it."

"You've seen it all before?"

"Yes."

"With your wife?"

He nodded. "But not the islands. They're strung out like stepping stones between here and Dubrovnik, all along the coast. I'm starting with Hvar myself, which I can justify historically, but it also claims to be the sunniest island in the Adriatic. I'm going to stuff myself with fish, curl up on a rock like a snake and . . ." He laughed at himself.

"It sounds lovely."

"Come with me," he said.

It was an idle response, offhand. She laughed to prove that she understood the joke.

"Why not? Seriously," he said.

There were dozens of reasons why not, all of them flimsy, trite, stuffy, hypocritical or silly, she saw, as Paul demolished them one by one. He had not propositioned her. She would pay her own way. If she was short of funds, he would advance what she needed. She could have money sent to Dubrovnik, repay him there before she picked up her flight home.

"It's up to you, of course." He let go easily. "It was just a thought."

Her misgivings seemed almost insulting. He had made a friendly, open suggestion. He was not trying to talk her into anything . . . or seduce her. *Honi soit,* she mocked herself. Little old Allen Whitcomb was far more prurient.

"You don't have to decide now," Paul said. "No hurry."

In the morning she spoke to Ivo and, hearing herself, the bald announcement that she would not be going on with the tour, felt that his astonishment could hardly be greater than her own. It was not as if she had thought the matter through or agonized over it during the night. She had in fact put Paul's suggestion out of her mind as unthinkable—away from him it had no reality —and wakened knowing that she had no choice, she was staying with him.

"My dear!" Ivo wrung her hand between his own, devastated. He blamed himself for some unspecified failure. He worried, dark eyes melting, because he would not be able to help her; put crassly, he could not refund her money, he had no authority. Marianna's reassurance was Paul's, ready-made and quick, perhaps almost too glib.

Ivo's manner changed just a shade. He was still unhappy, but his concern lay in another direction, away from his professional responsibility. He had quite probably seen her with Paul—or heard the ladies clucking. "It is not my place," he began.

"No." She did not want his advice, the other side, to

be unsettled again. She smiled to soften her bluntness. "I'm old enough."

He shrugged tactfully, conceding, but dissatisfied still. Marianna felt his eyes on her several times during breakfast and thought that he had something further to say, but if he did, he refrained.

She saw him once more, a little later, in the lobby. The island of American suitcases had reappeared. The tour group jammed the elevators and the souvenir counter. Ivo dashed back and forth, pulled in all directions like a sheepdog whose flock has stampeded. He stopped and said, *"Dovidjenja,"* sweetly, holding Marianna's hand, and translated into self-conscious American slang: "So long. I'll see you."

"Of course. At the airport in Dubrovnik. You can wave me off home. Say good-bye to the others." She did not want to have to explain; she was not sure that she was strong enough to withstand either disapproval or coy approval. She could well imagine Mr. Whitcomb's assumptions—turned nasty by envy—and Miss Hawthorne crackling with malice, feeling her own pleasures devalued.

The bus was thrumming outside the door, smelly. Marianna hurried around it onto the sunny promenade that curved back into town. The blue water sparkled, roughed up by a slight breeze. The terra cotta roofs were rosy, the pale stone buildings bleached almost white in the clean morning air. It was as she stood at the curb waiting to cross that the tour bus went by. She had a blurred, watery impression of heads behind the tinted glass, floating past in their aquarium. She did not think that they saw her—already she felt assimilated into the landscape. Anyway, nobody waved.

Paul had said that he walked downtown every morning to buy the *Herald-Tribune.* He would read it in the sun while he drank *cappuccino* at one of the sidewalk cafés facing the harbor. She searched through the little tables with sudden anxiety, not seeing him. What if he were not there . . . if she had misunderstood . . . or if he had had second thoughts?

What if he, too, had left? The wordless questions broke over her all at once like a giant wave. She felt herself sinking, dragged down and swirled about in the undertow.

And then she saw him, the now-familiar shape of his large shaggy head. She waited until she could speak calmly.

"Good morning."

"You're late." He half-smiled and stood up to pull out a chair for her. "They start early around here. After about ten o'clock they don't consider it morning any more. They switch to 'Good day.' "

"Good day," she said, trying to match his level tone, not laugh aloud. "It *is* a good day."

"Your gang gone?"

She nodded, nervous excitement rising like bubbles. She was almost thirty years old and could barely control giggles. That in itself was absurd.

Without asking, Paul ordered *cappuccino* for her. "When you've finished that," he said, "we'll get your

22

banking business out of the way and hop a bus to Trogir." He folded his newspaper and filed it in his jacket pocket.

The little cup of milky coffee was warm in her hand. She felt snug and sure. As long as Paul knew where they were going and made all the decisions, she felt marvelously competent. "I'm ready."

They stood up, scattering a flock of crumb-hungry pigeons, brown ones or brown and white.

"Look, Paul!" She had never seen brown pigeons before.

"I know. Stick with me," he said grandly. "You ain't seen nothing yet."

Chapter 3

The bus lurched and spluttered like a city bus any-where. Marianna would have sat down—there was room on the side seat at the front—but she was elbowed aside by an indignant man. Not a gentleman; she turned to Paul with indignation.

He was laughing. "Unless you're pregnant. The front is reserved for the elderly and invalids, or people with children. Or pies," he amended as a pink-faced chortling woman patted the box on her lap.

The passengers were easily amused. They looked well fed, generally chunky, a little dowdy. Standing and swaying, unable to see out the windows without painful contortions, Marianna studied them. There was one other woman in pants, and when the man next to her wanted to get off, he pushed her legs aside as if she were a boy, apparently assuming that she was a boy—his consternation was elaborate.

Paul, swaying next to her, saw the same things that she saw. They would exchange glances, sharing, finding conversation unnecessary. Marianna found herself smiling a great deal. She could think of nowhere in the world where she would rather be, and was jolted by superstitious awe at the enormity of her contentment.

By the time that they arrived at Trogir, she felt that she had memorized all the faces on the bus and would have recognized them anywhere, like old friends. Beyond simple curiosity about obvious foreigners, she was sure that none of them was particularly interested in her, or in Paul. She would have noticed and remembered. She was all eyes, like a camera, minutely recording, but all her images had a golden cast and softened edges.

She tried to express something of this when, bracing for their assault on Trogir, as Paul put it, they were seated at a sun-dappled café table just outside the tiny town.

"You mean slightly out of focus?" he said. "Nicely blurred? From drinking wine in the sun maybe?"

"Before that. I've never been . . . well, happier." It was not quite what she had meant to say. She was thinking how secure she felt with him, and strong. Even with Ted she had never felt so protected. But then, in those days, there had been no need; she had been so strong within herself, so confident.

"I'm glad." Paul spoke quickly, as if to stop her from saying anything more. "Now, madame, for the personally conducted, custom-tailored, A-number-one tour of medieval Trogir."

She floated through the ancient narrow lanes into the square and the loggia and the aisles of the cathedral, wherever Paul suggested, seeing whatever he pointed out. Here, too, laundry was strung through the town like pennants, as proof of occupancy, and there were children and cars and garbage. The shops had odd little doorways, comma-shaped. Magenta snapdragons sprouted improbably from the walls. She retained all these impressions vividly with heightened senses, feeling enormously alive. She would have been aware, surely, if anyone had been watching them or paying undue attention.

Anyone but the friendly young waiter. They went back to their café for lunch with a proprietary attitude, returning to their old table. Paul ordered omelets and more of the pale yellow wine.

"No, I find it the least sinister of countries." Paul even said that at one point, she remembered. "Live and let live . . . young in spirit . . . safe." She remembered his exact words and had no reason to doubt them.

"And tomorrow," he said, "we'll start island-hopping."

A battering wind whipped the kerchief she had tied around her hair. The high sun was blinding on the open upper deck. Marianna closed her eyes, sliding lower on the slatted bench, and gave herself up to the sensation of the ventilating wind and the pulsing boat pitted against the sea. The voices around her were blown away. They were incomprehensible in any case, speaking Serbo-Croatian. Only the recurrent *dobro*—meaning good, well, fine; you can just toss it in anywhere as a friendly gesture, Paul had instructed her—came through.

More restless than she was and curious about the boat itself, Paul roamed the two rather limited decks. At intervals he reported back. Most of their fellow passengers were below, it seemed, huddled in out of the wind. The land on the left was Brač. Idly Marianna wondered why they did not get off there, but Paul was in charge; it did not occur to her to question his decisions. Hvar would be next, he said, a long skinny island. The town of the same name, where they were going, was just around the tip on the other side.

Marianna stood by the railing watching the little red-roofed town materialize, the nearly white sun-struck buildings and the palm trees waving like giant fans behind the stone pier. Her first impression, she was to remember, was one of delight.

As the engines reversed, churning the royal blue water into a pale turquoise forth, she went below to find Paul. He was by the lower rail with his back to her, talking to someone, a man. And then the gangplank was being readied, there was a general rush to this side, and the man was gone.

"Who was that?"

"Who? Oh, him. No one you'd want to know."

"You knew him before?"

"Yeah."

She regretted her question. Paul looked annoyed, lips compressed, as if she had been prying. But before she could apologize, the unpleasant moment was over. A noisy phalanx of tourists, eager to disembark, flattened them against the railing. Paul made a guttural protest, laughing, and entered into a good-natured wrangle.

"You speak German, too?" she said.

"Some. It comes in handy. It's pretty much the second language around here."

"A man of many talents."

"But master of none," he murmured, oddly flustered.

Hidden talents, Marianna thought, the words lodging unwanted in her mind. She still had such a lot to learn about Paul Currier. A lot; only the faintest misgivings tinged this prospect—and these were forgotten as she reached the head of the gangplank. The steep, unsteady ramp claimed her full attention.

"Oh, *yes,*" she decided, blissfully drawing out the word and spreading her arms as if to embrace all of Hvar, feeling that she could embrace the entire town. It was a manageable size, easily grasped, a tidy crescent snugged against high green hills. In a matter of hours she felt that it was hers. She claimed it.

They had walked it, first to their hotel with a porter carrying their bags the short distance from the boat landing. Marianna had alighted in her room just long enough to hang over her funny little blue, arched balcony and savor the sea and geraniums, the scattering of islands in her private framed view, and one small monastery. She was eager as a child to see the rest, to tear into it all at once, like a pile of presents.

Paul had made her sit down at last for an apéritif,

when they had come almost full circle back to an open-air restaurant beside the dock. A handsome sloop rocked nearby, creaking lightly. With evening the wind had subsided. The overhanging palms barely rustled.

"I *like* it," Marianna went on. "I have tried it on and it fits. It's me, the new me. Paul . . . seriously, you've no idea what you've done for me, how grateful I am. It's as if . . ."

She faltered as he lowered his eyes with an ambiguous frown that might have been embarrassment.

". . . as if I left all my uncertainties back on the mainland," she plunged on. "This is another incarnation. I'm a different person here."

He raised his glass. "To you, either one of you."

"And you."

This time he did not look away, but studied her face as if he were learning it. He reached over to weigh her hair in his hand and ran a finger along the curve of her jaw. It was Marianna who looked away this time, surprised by his intensity and the warmth it caused, like a thaw beginning in her own body.

The sloop was dark-hulled, dipping gracefully, emitting a rhythmic ping as a loose line flapped against a mast.

She was totally unaware of the woman behind her until the contralto voice rang out: "Boyd! Darling! I do not believe it. What you are doing here! I thought"—her staggering assurance cracked fractionally—"but you *are* Boyd Currier?"

"No." Paul said it pleasantly enough, but Marianna

29

sensed his control, the underlying effort to be polite to this woman. She was bright blond, deeply tanned, her skin leathery from exposure; and there was a little too much of her, straining her bright print dress.

"No, but I'm told we look alike. There's supposed to be quite a family resemblance. I'm his brother." Paul did not invite her to sit down. He had stood up himself in a temporary attitude.

"Forgive me! How stupid I am!" She was remorseless, however. "But of course. Boyd will be in Belgrade now." She put out her hand and shook Paul's aggressively. "I am Lotte. Lotte Ludwig."

"This is Mrs. Eames." He murmured it.

"Mrs. Eames," the woman repeated. There was a flicker around her eyes. "But I am interfering. Paul . . . I may call you Paul? I am keeping you standing. You must sit down. Forgive me."

If you're stuck anyway, if there's absolutely no way out, Marianna had learned long ago in Washington, you might as well be gracious. Paul apparently had reached the same conclusion. Lotte was seated and three drinks were ordered.

"You have not been here long?"

"No," said Paul.

"So . . . you have very much to see." Her circling hands were heavy with rings. Her accent, also fairly heavy, Marianna could not be sure of. German perhaps . . . or Slavic?

"You have climbed to the fortress, yes?"

"No," Marianna said.

30

"But you must. It is most interesting, most historic. From the sixteenth century. You will admire the old walls—from the Middle Ages, some of them are—and the gardens. And now it will be a restaurant up there. And the view, all this"—her gesture encompassed the bay—"is like toys, you understand? The miniature, the child's village made of blocks?

"All the island is good. You will go to Stari Grad, yes? To the palace of the poet Hektorović."

There was a kind of rapture in her hands and face. Or, Marianna thought coldly, salesmanship, a shade of Connecticut Avenue boutiques about Lotte's enthusiasm? Lush and perfumed, Lotte was definitely a man's woman; Marianna found herself looking around for the man who should have been with her.

"Poets had it better in those days," Paul said dryly.

"Oh, yes! You have seen the monuments. They are much honored, the poet . . . the composer." Lotte smiled uncertainly and returned to the surer ground of her own subject. "All the cultures through the ages, they have been here. The Greeks and the Romans, the French, the Venetians, you will see the . . . the evidence? Even before that—before history!—the caves of the Stone Age. But you know all this." Lotte beamed the full force of her personality at Paul.

"And your brother . . . he is well? He is pleased with his . . .?" She fluttered her hands as if the word, like a darting insect, eluded her.

"His new post? I imagine so, yes," Paul said.

"You have seen him? Recently?"

"I thought I'd give him a chance to settle in, probably swing around that way later, before I leave the country anyway."

"You are not close." Lotte's face puckered.

Paul shrugged. "We're brothers. Anglo-Saxon. Not effusive, shall we say?" He smiled, softening this. "We fought like tigers when we were kids, now we get along well enough. I think I could say we like each other very much."

"I see," Lotte said slowly, as if still sorting the meaning from his words.

She did not stay much longer. Their glasses were mercifully small, Marianna noted, and Paul did not suggest a refill. He stood up quickly when Lotte made her first move. She held out her hand again. "But we will meet soon again. It has been such a pleasure, to meet you, and the town is small. *Dovidjenja.* And you, too, Mrs. Ease."

There was a decent interval before Marianna laughed. "I don't know what it is about her, something . . ." She stopped short, in danger of sounding catty— or jealous, threatened.

"A little overwhelming?" Paul was puzzled. "I agree, and she's not exactly Boyd's type either. I wouldn't think so anyway, though I can see her freeloading at Embassy soirees, one of the international lot." He was unusually harsh and, as if hearing this himself, went on to explain. "It's part of what I'd had enough of, that life, when I went back to teaching. I suppose she and Boyd met in Paris . . . or Bonn, he was assigned there earlier,

32

and to a lot of other European capitals, for that matter."

"You didn't ask her."

He laughed, a little shamefaced. "I was afraid she'd tell me—at length. Shall we go? They'll be serving dinner back at our hotel."

Walking back between the water's edge and the now-motionless palms, they did not mention Lotte again—she was clearly a closed subject as far as Paul was concerned—but she was there, lodged in their minds. Marianna imagined her forceful perfume clinging like a flavor at the back of her throat.

"I didn't know your brother was in Belgrade," she said at dinner in a low voice, somewhat daunted by the starchy little dining room.

"As Ambassador yet, or about to be. I don't know if he has taken over officially, presented his credentials to the President and all that. It's a good appointment. He's a career officer, dedicated, correct."

"And looks like you."

"So it seems. We've been mistaken for each other before. I'd hoped, now that I've fattened up my hair and cultivated sideburns beyond the prescribed limits allowed by protocol . . ." He laughed. "Red wine with your *Wiener schnitzel?*"

The food, like the voices around her, was Teutonic. Many of the fair complexions were ablaze with painful sunburn. Unhampered by facts in that idle game that is best played among total strangers, Marianna speculated widely, assigning professions, athletic prowess and attitudes at will, although in a whisper. "Do you notice a chill? I feel very like the new girl at school, being looked up and down."

"Have you ever braved a British club? Or boarding house? There's a definite pecking order based on length of residence—probably not as hostile as it seems. And then, we stick out as Americans. Foreigners. It's an idea Americans have trouble getting used to. At least" —he laughed at her softly—"you don't have to contend with your countrymen out here. I think we're at last out of tour bus range."

And very much on our own, by ourselves . . . Paul and I. A sort of tremor ran through her, not unpleasant. His strong face and steady hands—he was pouring wine again with concentration—were gentle in this light; she wanted suddenly to touch him, to trace the shadowed crease in his cheek. For his part, he gave no sign of craving other company. He had certainly not encouraged Lotte—on the contrary—nor anyone else.

After dinner, when there was a trend toward the lounge and the unmistakable blare of a television set, Paul turned instead to the front entrance. "You don't have to, of course, but I'm going for a walk. *Grosse gotte!*" He patted his stomach.

She did not consider not going with him. What else would she have done? They walked arm in arm for a time, adjusting to the darkness and the uneven paving.

"Like a proper, stodgy couple," Marianna said complacently. "I'd almost forgotten what it was like, how nice it could be, just being with someone, quietly. Like this."

"I know."

Awash in contentment, she thought and was almost afraid to say any more. "I've wondered sometimes if it's tempting fate, being happy. Too happy. Do you think I'm overdoing it?"

"Nope." He snugged her hand into the crook of his arm and smiled down at her. "You're just right."

"You may have saved my life."

"And therefore it's mine?" He was smiling still and his tone was light, but . . . that *was* how she felt, utterly and willingly dependent in a way that would once have horrified her. She had always been proud of her independence, her competence. With Ted . . . she had loved him, but never leaned on him. There had been times when she was the stronger, but never this—she had to grope for the words even—this welcome abdication.

The water made licking sounds against the wall and rocked the oars in a tied-up dory. Reflected lights wriggled in the shallow waves. Their silence, Marianna was keenly aware, was no longer neutral as it had been.

"Yes," she said at last.

But too late—or too softly. Paul said "What?" as if he had lost the thread, his thoughts had moved on.

"I'm so grateful. I didn't mean to throw myself at you."

He hesitated, then was unexpectedly grave. "Don't confuse gratitude with a lot of other things, Mari. Give yourself time. We've got plenty of time."

The lights of a bright little café crossed his face. Marianna could see that he was not looking at her, but at everyone else, searching the interior of the café and the tables out front. "A nightcap?"

"If you do."

They sat at one of the shadowed outdoor tables, not for long. Paul was impatient and when a waiter did not appear immediately he went inside to get their *vinjaks* himself. He was distracted, watching everyone who came by. She wanted to remind him, using his own words, that they had time, plenty of time, but nothing came out easily now, and then she thought that the only person they knew on the island was Lotte, and wondered if there might be a connection, if he could be watching for her.

"All set?" He had finished his drink in two swallows.

She gulped hers and stood up obediently, wanting to ask what was wrong, but the place seemed too public —and it was no easier away from the lights when they were walking back to the hotel. The tension—and it had become a palpable thing between them—only increased with the stretching silence. They walked faster. Twice, she thought—at least twice—Paul looked over his shoulder, glancing back quickly.

At the desk in the little hotel he picked up both their keys, went with her to her door and opened it for her.

"Okay?"

"Paul, what is it? If it's something I said . . .?" Her voice was wrong. Withheld too long, the question came out badly, almost querulously. She tried again, smiling. "If I was too forward . . . or something?"

"You? Never." He kissed her lightly and put his arms

36

around her at last. "You're lovely," he said. He held her against him, motionless, as if she were fragile or the slightest move might upset some delicate balance between them. She tightened her arms around him, afraid that he would let her go, and gave herself up to an extraordinary wave of relief that left her weak-kneed, relieved that he was back after what seemed a very long time away.

He brushed her lips again, then held her away and said, "Lovely," again, "Absolutely lovely," studying her face. She had no doubt what he saw there—her feelings must have been obvious—and very little doubt about what would happen.

But Paul shook his head. There was regret in his smile and a trace of embarrassment. He put her arms down at her sides with surprising force, as if she were a stiff-jointed doll.

"At the risk of qualifying for some goddamned merit badge," he muttered, "good night."

She watched him go; not down the hall to his own room, but back to the stairs and down, going out.

Chapter 4

The morning was cloudy and warm, weighted and troubling in a way that Marianna at first found difficult to analyze. She felt heavy and hung over—in accordance with whatever law it is that equates the heights of happiness with the depths of depression—and worn-out by dreams that she could not reconstruct. What remained was the totally black, totally negative thinking of the wakeful hours between three and five o'-clock. The safety that she had felt with Paul was gone, reversed somehow, as her first impression of Hvar was, the self-contained charm turned to terrifying isolation. The unquiet water kept reminding her: she was surrounded, out of her depth; she shouldn't have come here. These dismal conclusions dragged at her and would not quite let go, even by daylight.

By repeating the word "coffee" over the telephone in a variety of accents, she achieved a breakfast tray. This she carried onto the blue balcony, slowly. She did everything slowly, peeled the orange and divided it into segments, sipped the coffee, broke the roll into tiny bites, postponing the day. She let the shower run for a very long time. Only when the telephone rang did she hurry, dripping still and wielding a towel one-handed.

"There's a bus to Stari Grad in half an hour," Paul said. "Are you game?"

She was, in spite of the faintest misgivings, so faint that they did not bear examination. And there was no time, in any case, if she was to be downstairs, dressed and ready to go, in ten minutes. The fact that Stari Grad was Lotte's recommendation seemed insufficient reason to miss it, or a childish and perverse reason. Marianna had always liked to make her own discoveries; she would have preferred to now—with Paul.

"Good God," Paul said on the second stomach-flopping curve. "Now I know what we do when we meet someone!"

"Close your eyes?" Marianna had already closed hers, cowering away from the side of the bus that overhung the sheer edge of the narrow road. There was no shoulder, no guardrail, no room to pass.

"Someone backs down. In this case a small yellow Volkswagen. Think how we must have looked from his side!" Paul spoke with a certain amount of relish.

"The ladies on the tour bus squealed all the way, and that was a superhighway compared with this, two lanes anyway." Her palms were clammy inside her locked fists.

"Come on, trade places with me. I'll take the window."

Resettled, he put an arm around her. She could feel the motor vibrate as the bus labored uphill, the gears grinding lower and lower, the clutching brakes. "I swear that driver knows to the millimeter where his wheels are," Paul said, impressed. "The curve signs here don't curve, they square off at right angles, literally."

She looked past him cautiously at a forbidding, almost Martian landscape. What must have been solid masses of rocks had somehow been raked into heaps like giant gray molehills that sectioned off the dizzy hillside. "The hardy New England settler begins to look like a piker," Paul remarked. Here grapevines crawled over the steeply terraced clearings and fat clumps of lavender sprouted everywhere.

The spine of the mountain—Marianna thought of it as some razor-backed and hostile beast—was level for a short way. The sea, far below them, was spread out flat, harmless-looking and very blue now that the clouds had burned off.

Then they were winding down again, the weighted bus resisting its own momentum, heroically digging in its heels, Marianna felt. She looked straight ahead at the high back of the next seat.

"Has my hair turned white?" she asked in Stari Grad. She could laugh about it—with all the bravado of an airline passenger who has landed the plane safely— once she had been released from the bus and found herself on solid ground. Her pride of accomplishment was bounded, however; there was still the return trip to be faced.

"A little wine," Paul said, "and you'll be good as new."

"Oh, yes, please. You seem to have a talent for sidewalk cafés . . . and lifesaving," she added tentatively.

"Do I?" He looked sheepish. "We'll talk about that as soon as I've defended my *al fresco* title."

Unerringly, almost as if he had been there before, he steered her away from the narrow estuary of the harbor into a small, sunlit plaza. There behind a low stone wall was a graveled yard just big enough for one tree and one table, three metal chairs. The table was square, also metal, painted marine blue, Marianna was to remember. A corner of the mussed, grayed cloth had been flipped back by the wind. Behind was a small openfronted restaurant with a bar at the left side.

"*Voilà, madame.* I trust that ze table by ze wall will be satisfactory." Paul bowed deeply, ushering her in. They burst out laughing together.

With a carafe of wine the pale yellow of the sunlight on the table between them, Paul said, "Mari, about last night . . ."

She waited, unsure that she wanted him to go on, to say anything that might alter this moment.

"Please understand. God knows, it wasn't that I didn't want you. You must have known that. But . . . it's just that . . . I mean, any other time . . . hell!" His hands flopped open on the tablecloth. "Will you listen to me!

If my students could hear me, they'd die laughing. The garrulous old goat himself!"

She put a hand over one of his. "You don't have to explain."

"I want to." He was serious again and hesitant, watching her closely. "But when a lady has already had too much . . ."

"To drink? I hadn't!"

"To contend with," he amended quietly. "When she's been going through hell and has her own problems and doesn't need any more to worry about . . ."

Worry? The word struck her as odd. Feeling as she did about Paul, wanting him to make love to her, she could not think of this as a problem—a solution, rather, a beautiful and joyous solution; a restoration. Remembering how he had held her, she closed her hand tightly over his . . . and saw him blink, startled, brought back from a great distance.

He had not been thinking about her at all, Marianna realized—certainly not of making love, but of something unpleasant, or someone. He had shut her out, much as he had the night before when he had been suddenly remote, unaccountably restless, and she had blamed herself.

"Paul, last night . . ."

He smiled quickly as if to deny whatever she had seen.

"You went out again . . ."

He nodded, a faint, rueful compression about his

mouth, then lifted her hand and pressed her fingers against his lips. "It won't happen again," he said. "Fair warning."

"Promise?" Her own smile felt watery, unreliable.

"And so endeth the first lesson," he said briskly. "I hope to hell our friendly neighborhood bartender doesn't understand English. I think I'm better at middle-European history, if you'd care to switch to my lecture on the poet Hektorović, whose palace, according to my researches, contains an Olympic-size fishpond. In the sixteenth century . . ."

If she could have chosen a time to make last indefinitely, to slow down and preserve, this, Marianna knew even in the midst of it, would have been it. She heard very little of what Paul had to say about the poet Hektorović or the remnants of ancient Greek walls. She was watching his face and his level, deprecating smile, thinking how beautiful beginnings are, and anticipation. She hoarded her wine, sipping, making it last.

She was away from the table very briefly—certainly not more than four or five minutes. In preparation for their walking tour she went to the "Ženski" and even then found herself absurdly anxious to rejoin Paul. She was impatient with lipstick and combed her hair hurriedly.

Walking back through the little restaurant, she could see that the terrace was empty. The sun, high overhead, made a dazzling square of their table, which was bare now; their glasses and empty carafe were gone.

She did not sit down again. Sure that Paul would be right back, she stood waiting by the stone wall at the entrance.

It had become a beautiful, sparkling day. Like the sky, the air itself had cleared. The little square had a clean-swept, lonely look, tucked back away from the waterside life of the town. Or a pre-season feeling, Marianna thought—the first days of May were cool still for a summer resort. Or the closed and lifeless feeling of downtown Washington on a Sunday morning. Washington caught her off guard. What had been remote and unthinkable, but long past, rushed ahead of her. With a sharp tug of homesickness, she imagined being there with Paul. They might go back together. She pictured him with her friends. All this swept past her in a matter of seconds: the agility of the human mind!

The first prickle of anxiety began a minute or two later, very faintly. She turned back toward the restaurant, as if a closer watch would hurry Paul. The bartender, proprietor, waiter, whoever he was, had come back and moved indistinctly behind the bar, wiping and rearranging bottles on an open shelf.

When Marianna sat down, in what had been Paul's chair, the man came out to take her order. She shook her head, pointing and miming an elaborate charade. Misunderstood, she ultimately burst out in sharply enunciated English. "I am waiting for the gentleman. I wonder if there is something wrong. I think we should go and see."

44

His eyebrows remained high and baffled, wrinkling his forehead.

Marianna stood up then and led the way to the men's room. The barman shot around her and barred the door with outstretched arms. His face alive with consternation, he pointed an agitated finger toward the ladies'. The exchange that followed was ludicrous, exasperating, increasingly impassioned on both sides —the words coming faster and louder—and altogether fruitless. In an access of frustration Marianna pushed past the man. He was too polite or surprised to touch her.

In any case the room was empty. Paul was obviously not there.

"Where is he then!" She was shouting still. Motioning to the barman to follow, she marched back to their table to begin again. Urgently now and with her whole body she acted out Paul's part and her own, sitting in one chair and then the other, indicating his size with her hands, and the position of the wine glasses, the shape of the carafe. She felt by the end that she had reenacted every sip.

He smiled appreciatively at her efforts, like a child who is mystified by the entertainment but senses that some response is expected.

"Did you see him leave? Which way did he go? Where? The American?" An emergency store of French words came to mind—or Spanish; panic blocked her brain. The effect was the same. He showed her his open palms in a universal gesture of blameless ignorance.

"*Gospodja* . . ." Head tilted, scowling and concerned, he studied her. Marianna was made to think of another universal gesture: the finger twirled around the ear to suggest loose screws or missing marbles.

"You did see him. You waited on us yourself," she shouted uselessly.

He raised his eyes skyward in a prayerful attitude. He had tried, he had done his best, wasted his time, and they were exactly where they had started, going nowhere. This little must be clear to them both. He nodded in a sort of bow and retreated to his shelf of bottles.

Crazy foreigner. She could imagine him muttering just that. If their positions had been reversed, if they had had their impossible dialogue in Georgetown, at the corner of 30th and Q, say, and he had mislaid somebody, wouldn't she have thought that he was a candidate for a mental hospital . . . or, at best, not quite bright? She fought down hysteria.

The thing was to keep calm.

Her legs moved, but strangely, stiff-kneed and on their own like a child's little plastic animal wobbling down an incline by itself. Donald Duck. The length of the village, a cluster of stone houses looking down a long inlet. The main street was the quay itself, dangling an assortment of small boats. The poet's palace was closed, to reopen at three until five o'clock. Paul was not there then . . .

Not anywhere. She would have seen him if he had been anywhere around the open harbor area. She circled back to begin at the beginning.

The bus stop. There was a scattering of people on the benches, early for the return bus.

Their café. The man was waiting on someone else now at an inner table. Seeing Marianna, he stood squarely in the entrance and sliced the air with both hands in a rapid negative motion, fending her off, his whole stance hostile and braced against further trouble. Like a tough umpire, she thought, and there was no arguing with the call. She was out. Or Paul was.

Paul might never have existed. That was the waiter's attitude. There wasn't the slightest evidence that he had ever been there, not so much as a wine stain on the tablecloth.

She retraced her route through the town once more and back at last to the bus stop. When the other passengers boarded, she did, too. There was a different driver. No Paul. She sank into a middle seat and closed her eyes.

The road, the grinding climb and swaying curves and jolting stops, became pure motion. She gave herself up to it, not seeing—and in a way, not caring—letting herself be moved mindlessly, like seaweed deep down below the light.

Chapter 5

Shock produces its own defenses, a sort of anesthetic which makes for merciful numbness—and then wears off a little at a time, but too soon still, exposing the wound. The pain has not been diminished, only delayed.

Marianna knew this all too well. She remembered the numbness that had followed Ted's death and the slow prickly return of feeling. And much later, when she thought that the worst must be over, the clobbering reality of it . . . the finality.

But this. She couldn't have dreamed it, made up the whole thing . . . could she? Imagined Paul, out of desperate need . . . a mirage in the desert.

No! That was madness. NO. The word rose like a scream in her mind, and she opened her eyes. The bus was descending down the last woozy loops, like a plane tilting for its approach.

Coming back into the little port of Hvar was a kind of homecoming. Marianna knew her way. She could walk easily from the bus station to the town square and across it, past the church and the old theater, to the quayside, which would lead straight to her hotel. If she had had to ask directions . . .

But she did not. Having been here before with Paul, she moved with assurance—and a sense of his presence that would not let her push him to the back of her mind any longer. He was intensely real, walking beside her . . . and his voice was, especially his voice. Words, little bits of what he had said, came back to her.

"Lovely . . . it wasn't that I didn't want you . . . fair warning . . ."

Then *why?* she wanted to storm at him. Why say any of that? You didn't have to . . . to be polite! Why say anything if you didn't mean it? But if you did . . .

Why take off? Vanish . . . in that particularly cowardly and cruel way? Why take me all the awful way to Stari Grad . . . to ditch me!

Marianna wondered if she had spoken aloud. The questions raged so in her head, it was a wonder the people on the street couldn't hear them. There were a lot of people on the street now, promenading, watching each other. She concentrated on controlling her face.

The afternoon light was mellowing, tinting the harbor a pale topaz. Clouds were piling up along the horizon, and the palm fronds were stirring, turned by a storm wind. The sloop—the same sloop—tugged at its lines across from the café where they had had cocktails . . . where they had met Lotte.

Marianna turned in there and found an empty table

in a corner that was darkened by the palm trees. She sat with her back to the wall of the restaurant, looking out toward the boats. There was an incomprehensible menu in chalk on a slate fastened to the wall over her head and a garble of voices around her. She did not care what she ate, she only knew that she must have something for strength, and by pointing she achieved a bowl of soup and some bread and a piece of smoky white cheese. These she consumed methodically while doing her best to keep her mind blank, not to think at all, because the next thing would be to decide what to do. There was no one else now, no one to help.

If a memory of Paul's presence definite as a hand at her elbow had made her sure-footed through the town, his absence was something else: a great gaping hole she had fallen into, a crevasse cracked open by an earthquake. With the return of feeling, she knew that she had been seriously hurt.

She forced herself to chew the last crust of the bread and to swallow it. A terrible alliteration started up in her mind. She was all alone on an altogether alien island in the Adriatic. All alone, altogether . . . She ordered coffee, remembering that Paul had asked for the Italian *cappuccino*.

It was then, staring into the milky cup, that for the first time she realized that Paul's disappearance might have had very little to do with her. Hypersensitive and unsure of herself, unsure of Paul except that she had to be with him, feeling so newly reborn that she had no defenses, she had been egocentric as a child. But Paul was a whole person apart from her, he had had a whole life before they met and might well have had his own reasons for whatever he did. They had known each other a matter of days. She knew only that he was good to be with. But she knew very little about Paul Currier, and what little she knew—or thought that she knew—he had told her himself.

"*Gospodja . . .*" That strange word again. "Mee-sus," he sounded out carefully. The young waiter seemed to be asking if she wanted something more. He was dark-haired, friendly, with eager brown eyes—like Ivo's, she thought, and was rocked by nostalgia.

She shook her head and he put down the check. She had not had to handle dinars before and was slow about sorting them out. Guessing at a tip, she put down some extra coins and watched for his smiling approval.

When he was gone, she sat holding her billfold, fighting down panic. She had a few dinars left, a very few, and a thin packet of traveler's checks for shopping, but she had not intended to buy much, not even one hundred dollars' worth of souvenirs. There was very little need for money on a prepaid tour. And when she left the tour, Paul offered to advance her whatever she needed until she got to Dubrovnik. But here? If there was a bank, she had not seen it . . . and God only knew how she would have gone about communicating enough to cable. There wasn't even an English language newspaper to be bought on the island. Paul had said so.

One summer, as a child, Marianna had gone with her parents to visit friends on the Jersey shore. In the household was an older girl, tall and clever, with streaming blond hair, whom Marianna had thought admirable in every way and had struggled to emulate. Following her along the damp sand, she had followed literally in her model's footsteps, straining her own short legs to span the wide-spaced prints so that she would grow tall and blond and clever.

Marianna thought of this as she walked back to her hotel, retracing the route that she and Paul had walked. The night before, coming along this way, she had been serenely happy. And then, going back, there had been bleak constraint, Paul isolated in his own thoughts, next to her but off in that part of his life which she knew nothing about. Knew nothing about, and now had to find out about. All at once, almost as if some mystical directive had come from Paul's route, she knew what she was going to do first.

A vinegary brown smell crept around the empty reception desk. The woman who was usually there was in the dining room at the moment. She could be seen through the closed glass doors, arranging the guests' bottles of wine and mineral water on their assigned tables. Marianna slipped behind the desk to pick up her own key and—in very nearly the same motion—Paul's.

She skimmed up the carpeted stairs and along the corridor to unlock her own door first—preparing an escape route, she thought obscurely, in case she had to hide in a hurry. Her hand was shaking, her whole body quickening with nervous excitement . . . or fear . . . or guilt. This was absurd, she argued with herself, waiting in her own room, trying to be calm. If she loved Paul, she had every right to go into his room; it was the only intelligent thing to do. If she could learn something more about him, find some hint, some clue to what had happened . . .

What really did she know about him? That he had a good face and thick, springy hair and a talent for finding sidewalk cafés. He was gentle and patient; certainly he had not pressured her into coming to Hvar with him . . . or anything else. He taught history, he had been in the Foreign Service, his brother was Ambassador in Belgrade, or about to be. He was divorced. He . . .

Surely his room would tell her something more. She had to go in there. She had no choice. The deeply ingrained ethics of childhood did not apply. She had been indelibly taught not to look at other people's mail, or into their pocketbooks, or even to listen at doors. But now . . .

Once in the corridor, she did not hesitate. Before anyone could come up the stairs, she had the key in the lock of Paul's door and very carefully, quietly turned it.

The door swung into a darkened, airless room. Heavy curtains blacked out the French doors onto the balcony so that Marianna could barely make out the position of the bed and tables. Remembering the plan of her own room, she found a wall switch.

A terrible tidiness informed her at once, but she refused to accept the evidence of the bare wooden surfaces and empty chair and tautly tucked bed. She had to open every drawer and door first, and then at last the naked hangers and utterly depersonalized bathroom convinced her that the room had been abandoned and newly made up for someone else.

Chapter 6

But he had been there.

She clung to this one fact through the night, sitting there for hours huddled on her balcony. Rain spattered on the leaves below her and occasionally blew in.

She did not go down to dinner. She was not hungry enough to face the dining room, to walk the length of it and sit there alone. They would know. Somehow it would show. They would know that Paul had left her. Dumped her, rather, in the most humiliating way, by sneaking off without a word, as if he could not talk to her, she was incapable of understanding . . . or would have made an unbearable scene.

They would all know. He would not have gone without paying his bill. He must have told the woman at the desk . . . and cautioned her against letting Marianna hear? What pains he must have gone to!

A black wave of bitterness washed over her. The protective numbness gone, everything had a keen cutting edge; she was lacerated by memories of her own stupidity, and gullibility, her starry-eyed scramble for love! No, she had not imagined Paul. He was real enough. It was her romantic version of him—idealized, adoring her—that she had hurled herself at—a beautiful subjective lover. No wonder he had fled.

"It won't happen again." Paul's words took on a cruel new meaning. He had already known.

"It is sudden!"

"Yes." Marianna's tone was flat, discouraging. She did not want the opinion of the woman at the desk, only her help.

"It is too bad he had to go." She smiled, a cozy, inquisitive smile, edged with pity.

"He told you then," Marianna said. "He told you where he was going."

"His . . ." The woman's English abandoned her for a moment, then triumphantly returned. ". . . friend! He said."

"Friend?"

"Friend. Friend," she repeated impatiently and made scribbling motions in the air. "With the letter to give him the things. The things from his room."

"And he told you where they were going?"

Whether the question or the answer was beyond her, the woman shrugged. Marianna tried once more, very slowly, and heard herself pleading, desperation in her voice. Abruptly, out of pride, she changed the subject.

"What I wanted to ask you," she said, "is about boats. I must go to Dubrovnik."

"Dubrovnik! Yes. It is very beautiful. Tomorrow, in

the morning there is a boat to Dubrovnik."

"I'll need a ticket."

The woman nodded. "I will arrange for you."

There. Marianna said it to herself, but thinking of Paul. She had made a decision. She was all right by herself. She was going to Dubrovnik and might even catch up with the tour. In any case she would have money there, and she had her plane ticket home. Money . . . the gnawing doubt returned, centered between her ribs. Would she have enough for boat fare after she had paid the hotel? Would there be any left if she needed it in another emergency? And if not . . . ?

She walked, filling the morning, following the curved shoreline around the walled monastery and out past the stark new hotels to the rocky white beaches of the private villas. Then back again to the harbor and the center of town, with the sun burning through now, hot on her hair. So Paul had sent a friend for his things. How beautifully he had planned it all, so that she would have no possible reason to suspect anything. How clever of him.

But why? *Why?*

The old fortified walls climbed the hill ahead of her, and the fortress itself loomed on the skyline, a massive presence, hanging heavy. The very magnitude of the climb drew her toward it, and the time it would kill, and the energy it would consume. By exhausting herself she thought that she might stop this futile beating of her mind against unanswerable questions—like an obsessed bird battering itself against glass it could not understand.

She started fast up the steep and straitened passages of this ancient section—like someone running away from herself or hurling herself into the elegant remains, crowding her mind with crumbling walls and Venetian archways, the pink flowers spilling out of the crevices and delicate windows framing nothing now but the sky. Where coats of arms suggested ducal palaces, the ruins had been reworked into a sort of warren of ongoing life.

Marianna went steadily upward, slowed here and there by difficult paving. Alone and unable to speak to anyone, she felt totally isolated—and aware, aware of her own rapid breathing and mortality and a jolting sense of history, of time and doom. Not surprisingly, she told herself, among so much decaying beauty.

What she could not explain so readily was why at just that moment she should think that she might have made a terrible mistake about Paul. She stopped in the middle of the path, overwhelmed. What if she had jumped to an altogether wrong conclusion? If, under-rating herself, she had underrated him . . . misunderstood completely. If she had had more faith in herself, would she have reacted quite differently?

She went on, but one dragging step at a time now as she argued with herself. Above the close-built village the way widened into an easy ramp that angled back and forth across the hillside.

What if he had not deliberately ditched her? What if

he had been forced . . . if someone else had made him
. . . and he was in trouble, terrible trouble, and needed
help? If he had been kidnapped . . . a hostage? Words
that she had only encountered in scare headlines came
rushing at her.

Then she should get help, tell someone. The police?
There must be policemen on the island. And if she were
wrong . . . overreacting . . . making a fool of herself?

Like the path, her thoughts doubled back on themselves.

Back and forth. Back and forth. It was a slow, gentle
climb through here, but she was tiring, dragged at by
indecision.

Or, she thought with an odd shock of discovery, there
was Paul's brother, Boyd, the Ambassador in Belgrade.
Should she try to reach him . . . and tell him what? An
incredible story. But then, Paul's disappearance had
been incredible; he had simply evaporated, or gone up
in smoke, like magic. Paul's brother would be sure that
she was insane, if she could ever get through to him, a
busy, important man protected by layers of operators
and secretaries. Who did you say was calling? Never
heard of her. Marianna imagined herself struggling
through layer after layer, explaining herself over and
over again. It's about his brother Paul. Something
dreadful may have happened to him, I think . . . or may
not have. And the Ambassador, thinly polite, would be
furious with his secretary for letting that madwoman
waste his time. And Marianna would have wasted her
money, more money than she had.

Or Paul would be sitting right there next to him—groaning or grinning?—saying sorry about that, he thought he'd made a clean escape, he'd certainly tried.

But Paul wasn't like that. Was he? She couldn't have been so fooled, so wrong about him. She had thought that she loved him.

The top of the footpath widened into a driveway that led around the back of the fortress to the gate. Marianna forced herself up the last steps.

Here again the centuries-old structure was in use, not just as a sight or a lookout point but as a restaurant. On the broad deck where the cannons had been, and still were, facing the sea, there were tables and benches and a small bar. The view, as Lotte had indicated, was extraordinary. The town became an infinitely detailed scale model of itself, the red-roofed houses tinier than Monopoly pieces, the fishing boats mere dots along the white line of the pier.

She stood at the crenelated wall, looking down. At this height she should have been able to think with marvelous clarity—and perspective and detachment, she mocked herself—and known what to do. Once again she went over everything that she could remember about Paul, from the beginning. There were no answers this time either. Her only certainty was that she was parched and must have something to drink. Surely Coca-Cola was a universal word.

"Mrs. Ease!"

If she had not been thinking about Lotte a few minutes earlier, Marianna might not have recognized her.

The brassy hair was hidden under an orange scarf and her eyes behind opaque sunglasses which reflected the sky and, as she came nearer, Marianna's own distorted head.

"You see!" she claimed the view. "Is it not beautiful, what I told you!" Lotte did not look as if she had climbed any long, hot paths. Her yellow linen pants outfit was immaculate. "You will come sit with me," she said, and as an afterthought, as if she had only just noticed, "But Paul is not with you?"

"No."

"He does not care for the views, the—how you say? —the sights?"

The reflecting glasses were disconcerting. Unable to see Lotte's eyes, Marianna wondered if she was imagining other meanings, a triumphant note just under the surface. Lotte was smiling. "You will be comfortable here? The sun, it is not too hot?"

"No, it's fine, thanks."

"Then I will order something, some beer, yes?"

"Oh, yes, please. How nice of you." Her gratitude, Marianna knew, was excessive, and largely relief; it was so good to have Lotte coping—and communicating. She had been boxed in with herself too long.

"So much walking makes you thirsty," Lotte said when she came back, a young waiter following with their glasses of beer on a tray. She settled herself on the other side of the table, leaning forward so that again Marianna faced the double image of her own head in the mirror lenses.

"But you like it here," Lotte said. "And Stari Grad? You have been to Stari Grad."

"Oh, yes. That unbelievable road! I'll never forget it," she temporized, and then she could not stop herself. As people who are too much alone will, when given a chance, she talked more than she meant to. She had not expected to tell Lotte the whole story, but she did—in detail, from the beginning—with a certain urgency, as if it were important to make her understand.

And Lotte was an attentive listener, leaning closer across the table. She did not interrupt at all, but nodded quickly and made encouraging little sounds, sympathetic or astonished.

". . . without warning," Marianna said toward the end. "Nothing he'd said or done gave me any warning. If anything I'd have said . . ."

"I know! I saw you together, how he looked at you."

"So I couldn't believe he'd do something like that. I was hurt. And humiliated, I suppose it was my vanity." Marianna made a rueful face. "And then I had an awful thought, even worse. What if something had happened to him!"

"Happened? How do you mean?"

"If he was sick or hurt or"—Marianna fumbled the word—"kidnapped. Or something." The idea of foul play was too melodramatic, absurd here in the sunlight. "I even thought of calling in the police," she apologized. "Or Paul's brother. I wondered if I should try to reach him."

Lotte's shiny red mouth opened and closed.

"I didn't know what to do. I haven't much money. Until I get to Dubrovnik . . ."

"I think," Lotte said slowly, "you must talk to Jack. He will know."

"Jack?"

"My friend. Paul's friend."

"I didn't know . . ."

"Jack Dance." Lotte wriggled off the bench and gathered up the enormous basket that served as her handbag. A fashion magazine poked out of it. She seemed impatient, fussing at the wrinkles in her slacks, smoothing them out—or nervous. She had not finished her beer.

"Right this second?" Marianna laughed to cover her uneasiness. She could not have explained why she hung back, why she resisted Lotte's help. She held onto her glass stubbornly. "Let me catch my breath at least. And finish this. I'm not used to so much exercise. I don't think I can take another step."

Lotte's smile, too, was a surface thing; she was used to having her own way apparently. "Did you think I walked! No, I will take you in the car. If you are so concerned for Paul . . ." She turned her back on the view and, swinging her basket, started toward the stairs, knowing that Marianna would follow.

Lotte's glittery, ringed hands did not suggest competence; they looked frivolous on the steering wheel. Stiff-backed and stretching her neck as if to peer down the vertical drive, she drove with a concentrated frown.

"I didn't know Paul had a friend here," Marianna said.

"No? He did not tell you?" Lotte looked straight ahead, squinting.

"Of course, I haven't known him very long. Only a few days," Marianna confessed; and it was true, although it sounded wrong, her feelings had been so intense. "I suppose there's a lot . . ."

"Mmmmm." The road demanded all Lotte's attention.

Marianna studied her plump profile, the florid features and short neck and chunky mascaraed eyelashes behind the sheltering glasses. She said nothing more until the road began to level out, or at least became somewhat less precipitous, between the small detached cottages and garden plots that ringed the town. Chickens pecked among daisies and poppies and enormous roses.

"Tell me about Jack Dance," she said then.

"He will be at Four Palms."

"I mean, who is he? Where did you all meet?"

"Who . . . ?" Lotte's English seemed to come and go. She looked perplexed as she glanced away from the road then quickly back to it.

"I hope he speaks English."

"Yes. Of course. We will leave the car here, back of the square," Lotte said. "It is near." She was very definite again, leading the way through a narrow, high-walled passage that proved to be a shortcut to the main square.

Following her, Marianna was grateful again, reassured. Pulled back and forth by indecision, she had not moved at all. Lotte showed no such doubts. Bustling along on her rather short legs, she seemed to know exactly what should be done. Marianna let herself be carried along, gladly, with a feeling that she was no longer thrashing around but getting somewhere—and easily, by simply floating with the tide.

"There. You see? There he is."

"What good luck, or maybe not luck. You said he'd be here."

Lotte smiled vaguely.

The Four Palms restaurant was evidently *the* meeting place, central and popular, close to the boats which were the town's chief activity and entertainment. It was a place for the old men to gather, and shoppers and clerks and young families out for a walk with their children. It was, in fact, where Marianna and Paul had first seen Lotte.

Jack Dance was already standing when they reached his table. He was compactly built, a little younger than Paul, Marianna judged, although his hair was fading and thinning back from a high, bony forehead. His sun goggles were amber, his skin rather pale.

"Mrs. Ease," Lotte began, and his hand shot out with an almost Texan enthusiasm.

"It's Eames, but please call me Marianna."

"Okay. What would you like to drink?"

"Coca-Cola?"

He smiled and held a chair for her, seating her so that

65

she faced the water and that gently rocking sloop, the same one.

"I found her at the Fortress," Lotte said. "She said that Paul Currier is disappeared. Vanished. Like that. Pfft!" She snapped her fingers. "In Stari Grad. Yesterday it was?" She turned to Marianna as if for confirmation.

"Around noon. We'd only just got there and we stopped for something to drink, after that hair-raising ride . . ."

"She was going to tell the police. Or the brother. I said talk to you the first thing."

"Oh, God!" Jack smacked his forehead and tipped back his head with a great whoop of laughter.

Of all possible reactions, this was the one Marianna least expected.

"She was very worried," Lotte said in a reproving tone.

"Sorry." His accent was flat, almost American. "It's just the way these things happen . . ." He broke off. "Didn't Paul tell you?"

Marianna's expression was enough of an answer.

"No, of course not. I can see that. Someone obviously goofed. Or got their signals mixed, which is more likely." He broke off again to give their orders to the waiter. "One Coca-Cola, two pivos.

"No," he continued then. "Maybe not. Paul is so damned careful. Maybe he thought it would be better not to tell you. Safer, for you . . . and then things happened too fast. You don't even know about meeting him then?"

"I don't understand. Any of it," Marianna said.

"God, what a foul-up." He massaged his forehead as if working out a complex problem, then leaned forward and motioned with a finger for Marianna to do the same until their heads were almost touching.

"Security, you know. Walls have ears and that sort of thing. You never know who might be listening. Not that many of them understand English." He smiled. "Maybe I shouldn't even be telling you, but in the circumstances . . ."

He drew back so that the waiter could put down their drinks. *"Živeli."* He raised his glass, and the smell of beer was strong on his breath when he brought his face close to Marianna's again.

"You know about Paul's brother? And you've heard of the C.I.A."

She nodded to both.

"He may not have mentioned his connection."

"He said he'd been in the Foreign Service, but he'd left. He was teaching."

"True. Or near enough." Jack shrugged, smiling. "But in an emergency, he could be called on. He was here, and when it was his own brother . . ."

"I still don't understand."

Jack looked over both shoulders, a charade of caution. "Let's say he was needed to pinch-hit. We got wind of a plot against the Ambassador. They look very much alike, you know. Trim Paul's hair, comb it the way Boyd does and he could be his double."

"A plot? What kind of a plot?" Marianna felt herself tensing, the first prickle of fear as Jack hesitated.

After what seemed like a very long time, he said, "Maybe Paul's right, the less you know, the better, for your own sake."

"A plot against his life. Isn't it?" Marianna persisted. "So it's just as dangerous for Paul."

"Well . . . yeah, you could say that. But Paul can take care of himself. He knows what he's doing . . . a little diversion."

"But . . ."

He cut her off with a silencing motion. His manner hardened perceptibly. "We're not going to argue about it. Naturally, I can't go into details. The whole thing's highly classified. I've probably said too much already. You've got to realize that there's a lot more at stake than just Paul Currier. Or Boyd. I'm talking about U.S.- Yugoslav relations in general, which are okay at the moment, friendly, you know?

"In balance." He waggled his hand. "But delicate. Any time you get a Communist country and a democracy, it's going to be a fragile balance, sure. It's bound to be. And the Predsednik is very much his own man. He doesn't align himself with the Russians either. So we've got sort of a triangle. Like I said, a balance"— again his hand teetered, then abruptly flipped over— "which certain people would like to see destroyed. You follow me?"

Marianna nodded.

"It wouldn't take much . . . an incident, a slight unpleasantness." His mouth compressed into a tight, cheerless smile. "The assassination of the U.S. Ambassador to Belgrade, for instance. You can imagine how that might strain relations."

His eyes were obscured by the amber glasses, but Marianna felt them on her, unblinking, measuring her, missing nothing. She wondered if her face gave her away, if the beginning of her revulsion was apparent, and this new distrust. She looked down into her Coke, not drinking it; he would see how her hand shook.

"So Boyd needed Paul's help," she said carefully. "He knew that he was here . . ."

"Stari Grad is closer to the mainland. And not so . . . so public, you know?" Jack indicated the steady procession of people who amused themselves by watching the boats. As if he had in fact read her mind, he went on then: "It is essential that we be able to trust you —you can see that—we've got to trust each other. Otherwise . . ."

There was no mistaking his warning. His smile was narrow and sarcastic. Her whole body constricted.

"Obviously, you will not want to talk to anyone about this, the police"—Jack snorted at the thought—"anyone. And you won't try to reach Paul. That could give away the whole show, if anyone knew he was in Belgrade. There is only supposed to be one of them.

"Now," he said in a brisk new tone which suggested an agreement reached, "unless we have totally misunderstood your feelings, you will want to see Paul again, to meet him, as planned."

"Now that you know he didn't mean to . . . to escape you," Lotte put in. She had been silent during Jack's explanations, only moving her head back and forth so that the changing reflections of the sky glinted in her glasses. With the return to romantic ground, she gave Marianna a sentimental smile. "You will forgive him?"

"I wish he'd told me. I've made plans."

"Oh?" Jack's attention flickered toward Lotte, then back again.

"He knew that I was going to Dubrovnik. I have to. I'm going on the boat tomorrow."

So briefly that she might have imagined it, Jack Dance seemed unsure. "Oh. I see. Tomorrow," he said slowly. "So soon."

"I have money being sent there. I need it badly."

"Oh, well then, if that's all. No problem." He stretched back and grinned. "I can let you have all the money you need."

"No, no . . . I couldn't." Marianna felt herself drawing back. He was too eager, too anxious to help, insistent. Barely covered by the polite surface of their words was the strain, a sort of tug of war between them. Lotte sat absolutely still, and Marianna sensed that she was holding her breath.

"Where was I to meet Paul?" she said.

"I'll take you there. That was our arrangement."

"No. I'm sorry. Maybe later. I have to go to Dubrovnik first."

"Then we'll take you there in our boat." He maintained a chilling smile until Marianna said again, "I couldn't," stubbornly, shaking her head.

"I'm sorry, too," he said then, "but I'm afraid you must. You have no choice. Now that you know about Paul's mission, we've trusted you this far, we can't have you wandering around on your own, you can see that. It wouldn't be safe . . . for any of us." The smile was gone, and the casual pose. Jack Dance hunched over the table and his fingers clamped around Marianna's wrist. "Remember that," he said.

Her own voice sounded unnatural, childish. "I won't talk about it, I promise."

"I know."

She could not see his eyes, but she felt them on her as she had before, their almost hypnotic intensity.

"It will only be for a few days . . . if all goes well," he said. "You will get ready to leave. Our boat will be back soon. You will stay close to your hotel, pay your bill, turn in your boat ticket. If anyone asks, you've had a better offer, with friends. Yes"—he stood up, faintly smiling again—"with friends."

"It was you who took Paul's things."

Jack did not bother to reply. "You understand," he said. "You'll be ready." He put a handful of dinars on the table.

No, she thought. No, I don't. And I won't. But that was after he had left, Lotte hurrying to keep up with him, her basket bumping against her side. As long as he was there, staring, she did not think at all.

No! It was a silent shout in her head. And then, oddly, when he and Lotte had turned into the square and were out of sight, they became unreal . . . or her own reaction did, this unreasonable fear of them. She had been sitting so stiffly, holding onto herself in such a way that the muscles in her stomach and back actually ached. She had been rejecting their help, wanting nothing to do with them.

Yet, at first, she had been glad to let Lotte cope, grateful to her, relieved at being taken in tow.

And Jack had seemed open enough, up to a point, telling her about Paul's mission. She could accept the need for secrecy. Fantastic as the whole idea might sound, the papers were full of far less likely stories. He might well be telling the truth. Why was she so sure that he was lying?

Somehow, she had to get away without them. Once she got to the mainland, to Dubrovnik, she would be all right. She would decide then whether to call the Embassy, or go straight to Belgrade, or . . .

Marianna had pushed back her chair with a sense of resolution and reached down for the handbag at her feet. It was gone, and with it—bit by bit as she scrabbled frantically under and around the chairs and table, the totality of her loss struck her—with it, the last of her money, her passport, her identity.

"No!" This time she said it aloud.

Chapter 7

"No." The woman at the hotel desk shook her head emphatically this time, her professional tact stretched thin. "I am sorry, madame. That would be impossible."

"You'll get your money! Don't you understand?" Marianna clenched her teeth. She was not going to cry. It was bad enough already, her wild-eyed performance. They must think that she was demented. She could feel them behind her in the lobby, fascinated.

"As soon as I get to Dubrovnik. And the refund from the traveler's checks. You've got to trust me," she said, but without conviction. She had said it all before, twice, with increased futility. With the first mention of the word theft, in fact, she had lost any possible sympathy. There was no crime in Hvar. Theft, it was indicated with some hostility, might be an American custom; it was unheard-of here.

"If you would care to telephone . . . to your bank. I will . . ." The woman spread her hands stupidly, retreating behind the language barrier. It was no use demanding to see the manager. This woman was in charge.

"But that would take too long. Don't you see? The money couldn't get here in time. You've got to trust me. The boat goes tomorrow morning . . ."

"I am sorry," she said again, patently weary, and then she looked up, past Marianna, her face clearing. "Please, sir . . . maybe you can explain."

"Got a problem?" Jack Dance asked.

"This lady, she does not understand that I cannot lend her the money for the boat ticket. She has to pay for her room . . ."

He laughed. "Is that all? No problem. How much does she owe you—for the room? She won't be needing the boat ticket. I can take her where she's going."

"No, please . . ." Marianna began, but it was useless to go on. Everyone in the lobby, she could see, was relieved, delighted by this happy solution. They watched, smiling, while Jack counted out dinars.

"Okay?" He slapped down the last one and turned as if he expected applause. "Are you packed?"

"No."

"Then hurry up. We're in luck. The boat is back, waiting. On second thought"—he turned back to the desk—"let me have the lady's key. I'll give her a hand."

The launch made a wide, jaunty turn around the harbor and pointed out to sea. People on the quay actually waved. Marianna found this macabre—and Jack Dance waving back at them like a tourist in a chartered fishing boat, in high spirits. They just stand there watching me be kidnapped, Marianna thought, and they wave me on my way!

It was grotesque, and yet, looking back, there had been no alternative. From the moment of Jack Dance's arrival at the hotel, there had been no way out. Or earlier. Going back to the terrace of the Fortress, when she had run into Lotte. That, too, she could see now, was part of their plan. From the beginning they had taken no chances on her upsetting their plans. They had made sure of her, sure that she would not report Paul's disappearance to the police, or to the Embassy. Until Paul's business was finished . . .

"Relax!" Jack Dance grinned at her.

And enjoy it. If rape is inevitable, she thought, was the beginning of that line.

"What's the matter? Don't you like boats?" He raised his voice against the wind. Beyond the protective bay, the water had roughened and the little boat, struggling through the waves, was beginning to pitch. Lotte huddled in by the pilot. Marianna braced her feet and held onto the railing, watching the village recede until her hotel, the palm trees, even the dominating Fortress diminished into mere dots and then vanished altogether.

"Will you tell me now where we're going?" she said.

A blast of spray misted his glasses. He laughed and took them off to wipe them on his windbreaker. Uncovered, his eyes looked raw, pale brown under puffy, almost lashless lids. He squinted in the light, examining his glasses, then put them back on.

"You'll like it," he said. "It's got quite a history, nice scenery, everything. Where we're going is an island in a lake in an island, if you follow me. Believe it or not, there's a legend that Saint Paul visited it, but that's slightly moot. There's an Italian island called Melita, too, which also claims Saint Paul. Anyway, the church is well represented. The hotel used to be a monastery —this you will believe when you see it—twelfth-century Benedictine."

All this he said in a bland, tour-guide voice—Marianna thought longingly of Ivo—until the end. "You'll be reasonably comfortable," Jack said. "You'll enjoy your stay, and"—on a warning note—"you won't worry about leaving. It would be impossible anyhow. You'll see that."

There was something hypnotic about the rhythm of his words and the intensity of his stare. Again Marianna felt that he could read her mind, that any rebellion would be apparent—and put down effectively. She turned away from him into the wind and spray.

They were running along the long coast of the island, past a tiny precarious settlement on the very edge of the sea. Behind it the mountain rose straight up, steep as a wall, a harsh, handsome, impermeable land. Here and there the gray rock face had been cleared and terraced, impossibly, and the vertical fields tilled.

". . . only for a few days probably, until Paul gets

76

there," Jack was shouting into the wind. If all goes well, she thought. That's what he had said before. If. She turned back to him.

"What is he doing, really? It's terribly dangerous, isn't it?"

His smile bared his teeth. "Later. You'll hear all about it when it's done. You and a lot of other people," he added, amused.

Late in the day they ate bread and Trappist cheese and drank the local white wine called Grk out of paper cups. Lotte hardly spoke. As she had all afternoon, she watched Jack, deferring to him and letting him do the talking. When she had arranged the food on the engine housing, she sat on the bench opposite Marianna, and whenever Marianna looked at her, her eyes slid away toward Jack, who stood by the pilot, pouring wine for him and steadying his cup.

With all the makings of a holiday outing—the boat, the wine, the postcard setting; they were in a narrow fjord-like passage between steep islands—it was a weird sort of picnic. Marianna sat in strained silence, feeling the throb of the laboring engines. She ate very little.

And then it was dark. Scattered lights, faint as stars, marked the shore but there was nothing else, no clue to what was ahead, only the determined churning of the boat.

"Not much farther." Jack turned away from the pilot and stretched. "At least to the first stop," he amended.

"Then there's a slight portage and another little boat ride"—he seemed to take pleasure from the difficulties —"and *voilà*. Out of this world."

"It is very beautiful," Lotte said doubtfully. "Very..."

"Remote," Jack supplied. His smile gleamed briefly in the dim glow from the instrument panel.

Marianna had always had a horror of going blind. As a child she had peopled the darkness with terrifying shapes, and she would not play blindman's buff or pin the tail on the donkey. She could not bear the kerchief tied over her eyes, the stumbling and groping and dizzy loss of direction. Just below the funny confusion would lurk helpless panic; she would snatch off the blindfold, ruining the game.

Now there was nothing that she could do. Beyond the greenish, underwater light of the cockpit was a dense, threatening darkness. The boat slowed as if it, too, were feeling its way among unseen hazards. The single beam of its spotlight picked through the dark, finding nothing.

As the floor had tilted when she was blindfolded, the deck did now, in a sickening rocking motion. Marianna went back to the open cockpit and clung to the rail and at last saw a white sliver that was a dock.

"All ashore what's going ashore." Jack was the first one off. He offered Marianna an outstretched hand to help her—almost to pull her, bodily—over the wide, wavering space between the boat and the pier. The land itself, she found, did not feel solid but continued to move unsteadily under her feet. She could see almost nothing, a suggestion of small, closed stone buildings and a van, into which she was shepherded. Lotte came in after her, panting slightly.

They waited for several minutes, not talking, while the men brought the luggage from the boat and loaded it in. Then the boat's engines roared in the silence and Jack climbed into the driver's seat of the van. "All set?" He adjusted the mirror and examined the controls, whistling softly between his teeth, then turned the key and started off into the night.

From the middle of the van where she and Lotte were sitting, Marianna could not see the road ahead, only some obliquely lighted, dusty shrubs at the edge of what seemed to be an unbroken pine forest. She could not gauge the distance . . . two miles, five? There was no demarcation, rather a sense of endless repetition of flat, sandy woodland as if they were circling the interior of Maine. Jack took the rough surface with a certain amount of caution. Lotte had put her head back and closed her eyes . . . asleep, or praying, or averting questions?

When ultimately they did stop, they were again drawn up at a dock so that it seemed possible that they had indeed come full circle, except that this was a smaller dock, and the boat a dory with an outboard motor. Jack left the headlights on, directed at the landing, until he had moved their suitcases out of the van and piled them into the little boat.

Then there was only his flashlight. He pointed with it to the thwarts where they were to sit, narrowly perched in the spaces left by the luggage. "Sorry, but it won't be for long. It's not too much farther, just one mo' ribber to cross—or lake." His false tour-guide jollity was wearing thin. He said very little more and in any case could not have been heard above the rattly, coughing motor. Lotte held the flashlight while he fussed with the starter, then he took it back and clamped it between his knees, flicked off.

There were no stars. Again Marianna felt blinded, lost, so tight with uncontrollable dread that she flinched when Lotte tapped her arm with a long fingernail and, pointing, said, "You see?"

Pupils dilated by the darkness, she could just discern a meager yellowish light, then another, like two faint candle flames. This impression of grudging light remained. Not candles but low-watt bulbs, wide-spaced, hinted at the looming shape of the monastery.

No one met them at the landing. Jack had bumped alongside and hopped ashore to tie up before anyone appeared, and then it was a tall, slow, long-armed man, slightly hunched.

"Nico?"

Apparently he was. With a suitcase dangling at the end of each of his long arms, he led the way: across a wide stone terrace, up wide, dark stone steps, through a sort of reception area which, however, implied no hospitality. In the conversion of the monastery into a hotel, few traces of its earlier austere function had been lost. Marianna could well imagine silent Benedictines shuffling along this corridor, enclosed in prayer.

Or on their knees in this cell. The vaulted white plaster walls outreached the tiny hooded lamp beside the cot. There was one high square window and, except for an adjoining bathroom with a makeshift shower, nothing to detract from the daunting authenticity.

Jack surveyed the room with satisfaction. "I guess you've got everything. You won't need a key. There's no one else here."

"I thought you said it was a hotel."

"Well, yes. In the summer," he said. "The season hasn't started yet. We're a little early."

Yes. The dank winter cold was still trapped in the walls—that lifeless, steely cold which penetrates the bones. The bedding, the rough sheets and blankets and mattress, hoarded old dampness. Marianna was shaking. She should have had a hot drink, or brandy, but Jack had left, there was no telephone—certainly no room service; she fought down tearful giggles at this idea—and she could not force herself to explore that long, blind hallway.

She did not undress, but huddled under the blankets in her slacks and sweater and constraining jacket. Half sleeping, she could imagine herself in some long-ago, long-closed summer cottage in Maine. She conjured blueberry bushes and sand and wood smoke to shut out the truth. The thing was not to think about Paul. He would not be coming here, ever. She *knew*. He had never planned to meet her here. It was all part of an elaborate lie. Nothing that Jack said could be trusted, she knew . . . but what about Paul? If he and Jack were friends, in on this together . . . ?

She lay rigid and cramped, knowing that she was at the end of the world, afraid of what the morning light would reveal.

Chapter 8

Her drawn-up knees ached. She felt rumpled and gritty-eyed and a leaden indifference to her surroundings. The fact that it was morning came into the cell at second hand, not so much a brightening as a lesser darkness. It was a long time before Marianna explored it further. Then she stood on the cot, arms braced on the deep window ledge.

What she looked out on was the cloister, the monks' enclosed walkway and raised rectangular garden, now a weed patch crossed by a sagging clothesline. By stretching her neck she could see a wedge of brilliant blue sky.

It was this and gnawing hunger that at last took her out of the wintry cell. And then for a moment she thought that a trick had been played on her, a dazzling theatrical stunt achieved with brilliant lighting. The somber corridor of the night before had become a wall of windows that framed great squares of summer sky. Below, on the terrace by the boat landing, a breakfast table set with a fluttery yellow cloth basked in sunlight.

Nothing else suggested the presence of people. The boat rocked lightly, relieved of its motor and oars. Nearby a mallard duck serenely laid an egg and strutted off with her mate. It was unreal: a stage setting, yes.

She went on, unsure of the way, but winding downward. Outside, away from the thick and clammy walls, there was a dense, almost midsummer heat. Marianna took off her jacket, too warm already, and at the same time began to doubt her senses. The aching cold of the night began to seem like a bad dream—and with it all of her unresolved fears. Her certainty of disaster, engulfing at the time, became a hollow memory, no longer quite convincing, like pain.

It was possible that Paul would come here, that Jack was telling the truth. She could almost believe that now, almost . . .

She had not realized that she was being watched. The man called Nico came out of a shadowy arch, a tray looking awkward in his hands. He murmured something as he plunked it onto the table. (*Dobro, dober?*—she thought longingly of Paul, who would have known.)

"Thank you. But where is everybody?"

He did not understand, and he hurried away from further questions.

An orange and a roll, a pot of coffee and one of hot milk, and a boiled egg. Soft-boiled, so Nico, or someone, must have known her every move and timed her breakfast accordingly. The emptiness, then, and her sense of total solitude were illusions, too.

The water licking at the rim of the terrace was ripply

and clear like a high northern lake, quietly sparkling. Cold to the touch; after breakfast she trailed her fingers in it and decided against swimming. She would walk instead.

The dark arches led into a series of low-vaulted rooms, in effect a stone-lined tunnel piled with tables and chairs. Marianna had seen that much when she met Nico and an inquiring look—not at all the look of a solicitous hotelkeeper; he was resentful somehow and defensive.

She flushed and said, "I'm just looking," idiotically, and turned away. She was too warm in sweater and slacks but unwilling to go back into her bedroom.

She followed the outer walls of the monastery instead, the pockmarked pillars and shiny hedges, their waxy white blossoms heavy-scented as gardenias. There were rabbits everywhere, black ones and white ones and every shade of gray, and nests of babies. A rough path led to a tiny chapel, then wound on around the island. She picked her way among the rabbit pellets. Trapped here on this island, unable to escape, she thought, they would soon overrun it.

Uneven steps brought her to an unexpected burial ground, the graves of a woman and her two daughters. Unaccountably chilled, she was backing away from the headstones when her foot dislodged a spatter of pebbles.

A sleepy voice said, "Jack?"

Just below Marianna, sheltered under the brow of the slope, was a cove with a pebbly little beach. Lotte lay there on a blanket, sunbathing. She was lying on her stomach, brassy hair cradled on her arms, her buttocks ample white mounds. She raised her head and said, "Jack," again, more distinctly. "I'm here."

This time Marianna, too, heard the crunch of his footsteps approaching from the other side. She crouched behind a headstone, then flattened herself in the weeds among the rabbit droppings as he clambered down onto the beach. She could hear the scrabble of pebbles and the rasp of a zipper.

"God, I thought I'd never get that call through."

"I thought you were with her. I saw how you looked at her." Lotte's tone was sulky, teasing.

Jack laughed, gratified. "I wouldn't mind, I can tell you. But that's business, baby, strictly business." There was the sound of a slap and a squeak of protest. "Got to keep her in mint condition . . . for a while, anyhow."

"What did they say? Is it done?"

"Tomorrow morning, eleven o'clock. The appointment had to be changed. The Predsednik had something else, he couldn't receive our boy until then. Just as well, maybe."

"And then?" The undercurrent of excitement was unmistakable.

"I told you. The Ambassador is supposed to present his credentials formally to the Predsednik, only it will be Paul, of course, in Boyd's place . . . for security reasons!" The phrase seemed to amuse him out of all proportion.

"But that's not all, is it?"

"All you need to know, baby."

"Tell me."

Marianna could imagine the ripe mouth pouting. "Tell me, or . . ." There was a low murmuring and scuffling, over which Lotte's voice rose in mock fury. "No! Not unless you tell me."

"Come back here, you bitch."

Lotte giggled. "If you tell me . . . the truth now."

"The whole truth, and nothing but the truth? Okay . . . okay," he repeated. "That's better. You'd have found out soon enough. The kicker is in the credentials. You've heard of letter bombs. Well, in among said credentials"—a giggle caught at the back of his throat—"boom!"

"The Predsednik?" Lotte said slowly. "You will blow up the Predsednik?"

"It's a possibility, of course, but these things are unpredictable. There's no telling exactly who . . ."

"Then . . . why? I don't understand."

"Don't you?" He said it lovingly. "Think a minute. Whenever it lets fly . . . whoever gets hurt, it doesn't much matter. That's the point. That's the beauty of it. The main thing is that it will have been officially presented by the American Ambassador. Formally, *n'est-ce pas?*" Jack let out a great hoot of laughter, full of himself. "So that whatever happens, the explosion will inevitably be associated with official U.S. foreign policy. Inextricably. The repercussions!"

He lingered fondly over the words. "Get it? Everyone's going to think, there they go again, the C.I.A.

bastards messing around with other people's governments! Assassinating communists! You can imagine how the Yugoslavs will take it . . . there'll be hell to pay. And there go friendly relations with the West, with the Soviet Union looking prettier by the minute. . . ."

There was a long silence before Lotte huskily said, "Does Paul know?"

"Paul? Good God, no! That's what the whole song and dance was in aid of, the alleged plot against his brother, all that crap. He'd have blown the thing sky-high."

"But he'll guess. Won't he guess when he talks to his brother?"

"Don't be stupid. He won't get anywhere near his brother. His brother just won't quite make it to the audience with the Predsednik, that's all. Paul will, thinking that's his mission. And he may even get away with it, depending, of course, on when the bomb decides to go off. It's possible that he could be well away."

"But . . ."

"No buts," said Jack. "Paul will do exactly what he's told to do. Georgy will see to that. Any hitch . . . remember, we've also got his girl friend."

Marianna lay paralyzed in the grass, not breathing. Straining to hear them, afraid that she would be heard, she had not breathed for a long time. Their voices had dropped now into the unmistakable cadences of lovemaking. She ventured to raise her head, and instantly lowered it again. Lotte had let out a little gasp. But it was a gasp of pleasure, Marianna realized, and nothing to do with her. For the moment Lotte and Jack were totally involved with each other; if there was ever a time to get away from them, this was it.

Even then she scarcely raised her head but slithered her way out of the little burial ground, then crawled on hands and knees until she was well around the bend of the path and certain beyond any doubt that she could not be seen from the beach. Only then did she stand up —and in trying to brush the filth from her clothing noticed the bleeding cuts in her hands and the torn knees of her slacks.

Rabbits scampered out of her way. She was hurrying now, scrambling back the way she had come with no clear objective other than that she must clean herself up before anyone saw her and wondered where she had been. If they knew what she had heard . . . but she could not think at all beyond the need to wash herself and change her clothes. And avoid Nico.

Close to the monastery she became furtive. Pressed against the crumbling wall of the tiny chapel, she peered around it, making sure of her route before she went on, cautiously now, wary of Nico, and doing her best to compose herself. The heavy scent of the bushes and the shimmering lake were at the edge of her senses as a bitter kind of beauty. More immediate were her abraded hands and the idea of rabbit excrement, a disgusting film of it around her mouth—real or imagined, she wanted to spit it away.

She did not see Nico—nor, she remembered, had she seen him at breakfast time, when he had clearly known her every move—and now she imagined him fascinated by her peculiar behavior. She had been hugging the wall of the monastery. Reaching the entrance at last, she walked up the steps with all the dignity she could manage, looking straight ahead.

If she had had a key, she would have locked her door. As it was, she locked herself into the bathroom and tore off her clothes and stood under the full force of the shower, soaping and scrubbing herself, and hoped that the rush of water drowned out her shuddering sobs.

Tomorrow morning, eleven o'clock. Jack's voice rang in her head. The water was beginning to run cold, she had let it run for so long, and she welcomed the shock of it, feeling that it must somehow unblock her brain. Paul . . . oh, God.

It was a nightmare. She was standing there watching it happen and she could not cry out. The sound was turned off.

In her head she was screaming for help. Or praying, formlessly, pleading for . . . for what? An unspecified miracle. On her own—short of mental telepathy; the wry thought calmed her a little—she could think of no way of warning Paul.

The whole bathroom was drenched: the towel and the clothing she had dropped on the floor. The clothing was a new worry, as possible evidence. She stuffed it into the wastebasket for now, then briskly rubbed herself with the wet, flapping towel.

"Marianna!" Jack's voice was not in her head this time. It came closer as he opened the door of her room. "You in there?"

She had a childish impulse to be silent, he was so sure of her.

"Come on down," he said. "We're about to have lunch."

She imagined him smiling, sly and pleased with himself, but keeping his elation in check. The change in his manner was subtle, shading toward contempt—which, God knew, she deserved; he could not despise her more than she despised herself—for her stupidity, her gullibility. She had trouble keeping her own voice normal. But any hint of fear or loathing would give her away. It would be the final idiocy. Her one hope was to act as if nothing had happened.

"I'll be right along," she said and, clearing her throat, "Two minutes. But don't wait, you go right ahead. I'm just changing into something cooler."

"Okay. Get a move on. You women can spend more damned time in the bathroom."

She waited until she heard the outer door close, then unhooked the bathroom door and peeked around it to be sure that he was gone. Summer slacks, a mussed but clean shirt: her lacerated fingers were clumsy with the buttons. She took some trouble with her hair, brushing out the damp ends and turning them under. It seemed important to look exactly as she always did, and as she looked in the mirror, centering and straightening the part in her hair, she was pleasantly surprised that the damage was not worse. Her hair was brown still, her features unchanged.

They had not waited for her. They were hunched over their soup plates at the sunny table, and Jack did not stand up but pushed a chair out with his foot. Consciously rude, she suspected and saw a flicker of triumph in Lotte's little smile. The chunky eyelashes were demurely lowered.

"Well, you made it," said Jack. "How do you like our little hideaway?"

"It's . . ." No word came. She made Nico's arrival her excuse, drawing back elaborately while he put down the soup plate which, like her breakfast egg, seemed to materialize on the instant.

"It is very beautiful, no?" Lotte giggled. "And romantic?"

Stiff-faced, Marianna attempted a smile. "The monastery is certainly interesting. And remote. The monks really went to great lengths for their privacy."

"That's what I like about it, the privacy," Jack said.

"When the hotel is open, then it is different. And the food . . ." Lotte stopped at a look from Jack.

"But Nico doesn't manage it by himself surely."

"Nico? That clod! He couldn't manage a *pissoir.* He's the caretaker, that's all. He looks after the joint in the winter. Oh, he may think he owns it"—Jack tapped his forehead—"could be the solitude's got to him so he thinks it's his, but he's just one of a lot of worker-owners."

"Then why can't we have . . . ?" Lotte caught back the question as Jack went on: "I told Nico we didn't want people working around. Privacy was what he was being paid for. Absolute privacy." His eyes rested on Lotte, who flushed, mollified.

"Or else. Unless he wants trouble. Some people might not approve of his little deal. But you haven't seen the rest of our island, have you?" Jack continued in the same chillingly pleasant tone.

"No. No, I haven't yet." It was best to focus on the soup, Marianna thought, and be quiet. She could not sound natural, nor look at him. Nor at Lotte without seeing the soft body lying naked on the beach. She went at her soup with diligence as if to catch up and felt the warmth of it rising through her own body. Or perhaps that was the sun, or Jack's close study of her.

Having finished his soup, he busied himself with splashing red wine into their glasses. "You'll have to come swimming with us," he said, faintly smiling. "There's a nice little beach around the other side."

"Isn't the water too cold?"

"Frigid!" Lotte shivered with delight, slanting her eyes at Jack.

"But stimulating. You feel great afterwards."

Marianna kept her eyes on her plate, afraid that Jack would read her thoughts, her revulsion. The teasing innuendo was unbearable, their including her in their sex play as they had used Paul, exciting themselves with his danger. She could not erase the image of their two bodies.

"I don't suppose you've heard from Paul," she said, sounding wooden and abrupt, and heard Jack pause to organize his next lie.

"No, I . . . we probably won't. Until he gets here, I mean, in a couple of days." He was amused, relaxed, plausible.

Marianna put down her spoon and clenched her fists in her lap while Nico pushed new plates at them, pork cutlets and cabbage, with a sparkle of grease in the full sunlight. "I don't think I can eat so much. It will put me straight to sleep."

"Why not? Nothing like a good siesta."

Her throat contracted. The smell of the food was sickening.

"A little more *vino*"—Jack brandished the bottle again—"and we'll all sack out like babes. One more for Morpheus, hey? Why not?" he repeated, sounding somewhat drunk already, high anyway.

"No, no, not for me. Really." She managed a creditable laugh, fending off the bottle, putting a hand over her glass, and knew as she did it what a mistake she had made.

"Your hands!" said Lotte. "Your poor hands. What have you done to yourself?"

"Let's see."

"It's nothing, honestly." She clenched them again, but Jack caught her wrist and pried open her fingers. "I fell, that's all. I tripped on the steps, that rough stone . . ."

Jack glanced toward Nico, silently questioning, but

the man's face remained stony and uncomprehending.

"I was following some rabbits, not paying attention," Marianna elaborated. "It was stupid of me, not watching where I was going." She was a clumsy liar, and she knew now why a polygraph worked: her whole body was hot and hammering at this frantic deception. Jack must feel her pulse in his rough grip.

"You'd better be careful," he said as he released her.

But he was not through with the subject. He finished his lunch in a perfunctory way, anxious to be done with it. Marianna, grappling with her pork because it seemed all the more important now to act natural and untroubled, felt his eyes on her, then flicking toward Nico. He was curt in his refusal of coffee and emptied the wine bottle into his own glass, ignoring Lotte.

"And now for that nap. You've talked me into it," Marianna said as soon as she reasonably could. She even hazarded another smile. "You, too, Lotte?"

They went up the steps together, the two women, and it was then that Marianna heard Jack go after Nico —not the words, which were from a language she didn't know, but the fury, the eruption of his tightly held temper. Lotte, chattering, did her best to block out the angry sound. "So many rabbits! Are they not cunning? The black ones and the white ones, did you see?"

"And the dear little gray ones?" Marianna could not quite control her malice. "Tell me, do you always have such a big lunch? I don't see how anyone can eat so much—unless you always take a nap?"

"On a hot day, yes. And then sometimes a swim to wake up."

"Jack, too? Does he have a nap?"

"Oh, yes. Always." The laden eyelids dipped in another bitchy little signal of sexual triumph.

"For how long?" Marianna wanted to ask, but she felt transparent already and unsure of the limits of Lotte's smug stupidity. As long as she was preoccupied with Jack, possessive and competitive, and considered herself threatened, no matter how absurdly, by Marianna, she might be useful, an unlikely ally.

"What time do you think you'll go swimming?" Marianna said. "If you go, I mean, and if I wouldn't be a crowd," she floundered in an allusion that escaped Lotte.

The eyelids made another lazy sweep as Lotte shrugged and turned into her bedroom.

Chapter 9

How long? How long did she have?

If Jack joined Lotte soon, while Nico was still in the kitchen, washing up . . . would there be time, if Jack came up soon and Nico was slow in the kitchen? Marianna's head swam in circles, heavy with sun and rich food and wine. She wanted to lie down—even the clammy bed tempted her—but there was no time. She did not go into her room, but stayed in the corridor by one of the windows staring out at the shimmering water.

Nico seemed to be general factotum; she had seen no one else. Would he sulk and work slowly, smarting under Jack's angry tirade? Even in rebellion let Marianna out of his sight again? Or be all the more watchful?

She felt caught in some monstrous time mechanism, cogs and wheels relentlessly grinding toward her. In exactly twenty hours the new Ambassador's "credentials" were to be presented. The formal diplomatic ceremony, ringed round with protocol and symbolic of the good will between the United States and Yugoslavia, would go horribly, hideously wrong. The Predsednik might be killed . . . or maimed. And Paul, in twenty hours . . .

"Not napping?" Jack's approach had been soundless on the stone flooring.

"In a minute. I was distracted . . . the view."

"Yeah. Nice." He grinned, his hand on the doorknob of Lotte's room—but waiting her out, Marianna knew. He was not about to leave until she went into her own room, and when she did, there was something snide about his "Sleep tight."

She closed her door with a definite snap and heard the answering click from along the hall.

Now. Her hand had not left the doorknob. She stood frozen to it, supported by it, drained of the will to open the door again, to walk through it and do what must be done. Or what she had thought must be done. She wavered, weakening, suddenly exhausted—she wanted to lie down—then was pulled up with a shudder as if the power had been turned on again, an urgent rush of adrenalin. There was no time for indecision. They were talking about tomorrow—tomorrow morning.

Now. She turned the knob with an even, silent pressure, opened the door, closed it and skimmed down the long corridor. There had to be a telephone somewhere, logically in that bleak reception area by the entrance. She hurried in that direction, gauging the distance as she went and wondering how far her voice would carry. The monastery lay absolutely still in the torpid afternoon as if adhering to old vows of inviolate silence.

At first Marianna saw nothing. A heavy counter was backed into a sort of confessional alcove. The visible surface held nothing but dust. Only when she had edged around behind it did she see the old-fashioned telephone set that was wedged into an inner corner. She drew it out, hugging it against herself and crouched on the floor with some idea of blocking the sound waves with her body, with the counter, anything.

The initial click of the raised receiver was startling enough, the blast of her voice shattering. But ineffective; her hoarse, urgent whispers brought no response at all. A repeated jiggling and pleading ultimately activated a human but altogether incomprehensible sound. She fought down the normal impulse to shout in her own language and spoke instead with harrowing deliberation, forcing herself to enunciate, quietly . . . not to scream.

"The American Embassy. In Belgrade. Please." No, she should not have said "please"; it would only confuse the woman. But in fact the one word probably made very little difference, their lack of communication was so vast. "The American Embassy. Americanski? Embassy? Belgrade?" she repeated, and then again with what she intended as a foreign twist.

Then, "Is there someone there who speaks English? Ingleski," she improvised, wondering if she might find herself connected with the British Embassy. That would be fine. Anything would be better than this.

There was an ominous silence now at the other end of the line, no telling whether the operator was summoning someone who spoke English or simply abandoning the problem. Marianna controlled herself for several seconds before she burst out, "Operator!"

There was no recalling her piercing wail.

Probably, she tried to console herself later, it didn't matter. The telephone call was probably a doomed effort in any case. It was also more than likely that Nico had already heard her, he swooped down so quickly. He snatched the instrument out of her hands, directing an angry volley of explanation at the operator. Having received a scolding, he now passed it on, all the while glowering at Marianna as if she was being obtuse only to thwart him. A succinct gesture of his chin brought her to her feet and sent her back to her room.

It was good to be out of his sight. But no help, and she had wasted part of an hour. The time grinding on, twenty hours had been reduced to nineteen. And the one thing left to do would have to wait for darkness.

She lay on her bed, steeling herself—and, ironically, killing time. It would have been much, much better if she could have started this minute, without time to wonder if she could do it at all, if her resolve would last. But darkness was her only hope, and at the same time filled her with black horror: the blindness, the groping.

The rain started late in the afternoon as a random, wide-spaced patter on the leaves in the cloister. The thunder was a low growl in the distance, not yet a personal threat. Shadowy at best, the room only became murkier, greenish, like the bottom of a weedy pond.

Behind closed eyelids Marianna tried to visualize her escape route. The far side of the island, the cove side, seemed to be closest to the land. But they had not come that way; they had come across the lake a much longer way, farther than she could hope to swim. She would have to cross at the narrowest point, somehow carrying clothing and shoes so that she could make her way on foot around the rocky shore, feeling her way in the darkness. . . .

She couldn't, not possibly. Her legs turned to mush at the thought and would not have supported her if she had got off the bed. She would never make it.

And that, of course, was the final alternative: that she would not make it. She would not warn Paul, not be able to. Or not—she at last let herself consider the possibility—not even try to reach him.

The bloodless, limp feeling could have been relief. She had tried, hadn't she? She had made every effort to telephone. No one could expect her to do any more, to plunge into that icy black water and find her way through that dense black land. She would never make it. It was a doomed effort . . . and very likely unnecessary, she rationalized. Jack could have been lying. Or Paul might have caught on. Or something. Something would work out so that everything would be all right. Wouldn't it?

Marianna actually dozed off for a few minutes, or

floated off. That was the feeling, of floating like a canoe, battered by waves of sound. They were voices raised in argument, her mother's voice and her own.

"You're not going? You can't. Not in this weather."

"I've got to. It's important."

"It's too dangerous . . . not worth the risk."

"But I have to. I'm going."

"No, Marianna!"

"You don't understand."

"Someone will be killed."

"I know."

She woke up to the sound of moans: her own.

The rain had let up by dinnertime, but the terrace was wet and chilled. A table had been set indoors in the vaulted cellar where great oppressive blocks of gray stone, roughly mortared, arched low, close to their heads.

Marianna would very much have preferred to dine alone. She was given no choice, however. Only one table had been set and there, clearly, she was to sit, subjected to the full force of Jack's anger and Nico's resentment—the plates flipped at her, like spit in her face. Lotte's eyes wavered between the two men. She looked swollen and sulky, like a child whose party has been unaccountably spoiled.

The thin veneer of courtesy was gone—and the mocking innuendo, Marianna noted with a faint sense of relief. And we're like a ghastly family, she thought, yoked together at the dinner table, hating each other but inseparable. Contending with the fish on her plate, she could hear Jack chewing in the charged silence, stuffing food into his mouth with a kind of fury as if he were stoking his temper.

"I thought I made it clear enough," he muttered, spewing crumbs. "I warned you."

It was the fear in Lotte's face that startled her. Until then Marianna had not quite faced her own danger. Paul was the one who might be killed. As long as they didn't know that she had overheard . . .

Lotte had made a quick gesture . . . of protest or pleading?

"One more fool stunt," Jack said, and there was no need to finish the threat. It was plain in his flinty stare. He would be watching her himself now, watching for her second false move . . . and there wouldn't be a third. Even now, as if he were measuring her, taking the slightest motion into account, he was observing her awkwardness with the fish, following its uncertain progress, aware that she could scarcely swallow.

And enjoying his role, reveling in the power he held over her, Marianna wondered, hoping in fact that she would make one last move?

Yes, he would like having the whip hand. His cruel streak lay close to the surface and, she was sure, he would welcome any excuse to wield his authority. Certainly there was nothing, no one, to stop him in this Godforsaken place—and nothing, including murder, that he couldn't get away with. Who would ever know! If she vanished without a trace, who would ever associate her with this island? Only Paul, if any part of what Jack had said was true; and Paul might well be dead himself, blown up by his own bomb—or, at best, in jail for his part in the plot. In no position to worry about her, whatever happened.

It took all of Marianna's determination to choke down the food. She could not have said what she was eating. It was all the same, tasteless and dry in her mouth, but essential if she was to get through the night. She would need every shred of energy.

There was a sardonic quirk about Jack's mouth, as if he had read her thoughts. She lowered her eyes again quickly, doing her best to make her mind blank.

Lotte fidgeted in the terrible silence, picking at her rings and the neck of her blouse. "It's so close," she said. "The rain makes it close. How can you eat so much?"

Which makes us even, Marianna noted, grimly chewing. Lotte was evidently one of those women who find silence intolerable. Launched on weather and food, she went on about them at length, her voice acquiring a whining edge as she enumerated her complaints. "But it is true, Jack. Nico is a terrible cook, he knows nothing. It is obvious. Cooking is not his . . . his métier."

"He'll do." Jack's tone was flat and final, warning her.

"But if we have to stay here very long . . ."

"Shut up." Jack was splashing wine around again, spilling it onto the tablecloth. His tension was a tangible thing like a rubber band stretched to snap hurtfully. He was tired of Lotte, sated with her for now. And frightened, Marianna realized with a start: afraid of her stupidity and afraid of what Marianna herself might do. For all his bravado, she sensed, Jack was a cheap hireling, at the bottom of the pecking order. Not especially clever, he had been entrusted with a menial job, and he was expendable. If anything went wrong now, he would be blamed—and dealt with brutally.

She pushed the thought aside, wondering if any hint of it showed in her face, knowing that a frightened, inadequate little man could be the worst of all. The more desperate he became, the more dangerous he would be.

"You play chess?"

The question startled her. "No. No, I'm sorry."

"Lotte's lousy." He was restive, all at once impatient with the meal. "Nico!" He shouted it. "Get this garbage out of here, and bring the chessboard. We'll show them how it's done."

The next hours were another form of torture. Whatever his intentions, Marianna felt, Jack could not have designed a more excruciating pastime. Not passing time but killing it, she amended, by slow and agonizing stages. The two men faced each other across the chessboard with a suggestion of locked horns. From the beginning as he aligned his pieces—snatching the white ones, so that he would have the first move; he pointed this out with a derisive hoot—Jack made it clear that there was far more involved than the game. His vanity was at stake, his very machismo, and somehow—in a way that Marianna only half comprehended with a

crawling sensation—she and Lotte were involved, too:
less as spectators than as trophies.

Jack became more and more obvious as the game
progressed, jeering at Nico, boastful. "Now watch this.
I'll have him in six moves. Check and mate." He winked
at Marianna. Whatever he said and did now seemed to
be directed at her.

"Christ, man, aren't you ever going to move. I haven't got *all* night."

"He can't think when you talk all the time," Lotte
said.

"He's stupid without any help from me." Jack smiled
unpleasantly, his eyes sliding around to Marianna again
and his fingers drumming on the table.

Nico sat absolutely still, like a jagged, hostile wall.
When he at last made his move, it was apparently a
good one, and unexpected; Jack glowered at the board,
silenced for the first time.

When Marianna pushed back her chair, his hand shot
out. "I'm thirsty. I only wanted a glass of water."

"Get it for her, Lotte." He did not look up. A kind of
fury was building up in him as he faced the possibility
of defeat. It would do him good to be beaten, Marianna
thought, but might well be a disaster for everyone else.

Lotte had not moved. Her face was flushed with rebellion.

"Really. I need to move around," Marianna said
pacifically.

"Go with her, Lotte."

With a slight flounce Lotte led the way into a dusky

kitchen. Their dinner plates were by the sink, food hardening on them. "He's a pig," Lotte said, taking random offense. Marianna, Jack, Nico: all plainly irritated her.

"Jack hardly gave him time."

"They are both pigs." Wrenching the water tap, she managed to splash water on herself and exploded into a foreign tirade that made her outrage perfectly clear.

It was during this outburst that Marianna first saw the knife. It was on the drainboard, the finely honed triangular blade nicked and edged with rust. She glanced away from it instantly, afraid that Lotte would notice, but Lotte was absorbed, blotting fiercely at the wet patches on her dress.

"Who is he, Lotte? Jack," she specified as Lotte scowled.

Again the language difficulty became a kind of protective curtain. Lotte, hiding behind it, managed to look stupid. Or frightened.

"Is he American?" Marianna asked gently.

Lotte considered the question for some time and apparently found it harmless. She nodded cautiously. "One half, I think you say. His father."

"And his mother?"

"Was European. I think Italian."

"I see." Marianna hesitated, then ventured one more question as casually as she could. "Who does he work for?"

This time Lotte's reaction was immediate, but not quite what Marianna would have predicted. This was intensely personal, possessive, female. "You are so in-terested," she said tightly. "Leave him alone. You un-derstand? Now get the water if you want"—she con-veyed a good deal of suspicion about this—"before he wonders what we do."

They found the men exactly as they had left them, fixed over the chessboard like carvings. Their bent faces were in shadow, but there was no mistaking the determination in Jack's, the clenched concentration. His fingers, no longer drumming, were hooked over the edge of the table and white with pressure. Then, as the women came closer, it was as if something snapped: Jack's head came up and grinning wildly, he swept the chess pieces onto the floor. "Done! Kaput! We don't have to prolong the agony. Nico concedes. Right, Nico? Now how about getting us a drink? *Presto!*"

Nico's hands looked lethal, great fists jerking at the end of his long arms as he lunged. But Jack was ready for him. Quick as a cat he had slipped off his chair and well away from the table. He stood waiting, lightly poised, a small gun in his hand, and there was some-thing macabre about his leftover, static grin.

Nico recovered himself clumsily. For an instant Ma-rianna thought that he might seize the chessboard or the table itself as a weapon, but his fury seemed to have blinded him. He just stood there, his fists working, the blood draining out of his face.

"Make it *šljivovica,*" Jack ordered. "We'll have a lit-tle party." He kicked aside some chessmen, and as Nico at last capitulated and went shambling off, he shied the board after him like a Frisby. It crashed on the brick floor just behind him but Nico did not turn.

"Okay, ladies, sit down," Jack said, his dreadful grin intact, like old makeup.

The temptation was to drink heavily, as Jack did, to gulp the harsh brandy as an antidote to the poisonous atmosphere. After her first drink Marianna saw the cavern-like room as a tunnel in a mine, filling with deadly fumes. Jack had her glass refilled instantly. This time she was more cautious, sipping, moving the glass to her lips whenever Jack looked at her, but not really drinking.

The gun had gone back into his pocket. No one had forgotten it, however. Lotte was compelled to start chattering again—mercifully, Marianna felt; she herself could think of nothing to say. A jangling went on in her head as if the tensions in the room sent out their own discordant vibrations. Or the wires had come unstrung, shorted out by some crackling electrical charge in the air. She could not think anything through. Nervous strain, a tightening band of it, made her forehead ache.

Only one thing was clear: she had to get away. Aside from Paul, aside from anything, she had to get away from these people, away from this island, before the explosion came. Because it would come. The emotional pressure was palpable . . . and mounting.

Lotte, Marianna marveled, jabbered on—about plans for the morning now. She would pack a picnic, with her own hands, a feast, she elaborated with a contemptuous glance at Nico. They would go in the boat. But, no, they would not eat on the boat—she made a face; she did not care for boats—they would find a beautiful place on the other shore, a private place where they could sunbathe, because the sun would be shining. She demanded this, pouting at Jack with the implication that the weather, too, was under his control. The strong drink was blurring her features. She had draped herself around Jack and caressed him as she talked, attentions which he shook off at first, then tolerated—as unavoidable, he indicated; he shrugged and winked at Marianna—and ultimately reciprocated.

Nico sat apart, looking stony and humiliated, his empty glass tiny in his hands. The drop of *šljivovica* he had been allowed would not account for his glazed and bloodshot eyes. Jack had poured the fractional drink himself and kicked a chair in Nico's direction in an offensive gesture, much as if he were dropping scraps to a dog. To complete this picture, Nico continued to stare at Jack, barely blinking, ready for a kick or a hand-out, aware of every motion. And Jack was fondling Lotte with a certain carelessness, as if she were a lap-dog, a blowzy spaniel, Marianna thought. But this diverting pet dog idea was abruptly interrupted.

"Pour us a drink, will ya?" Jack had been watching her for some time, his expression speculative, and now there was the beginning of a playful smile as he looked from Marianna to Nico and back again, coupling them. "Your boy friend, too. I guess he can handle a little more and still function."

Oh, no. Please. It was a silent shriek. Any protest, she

was afraid, would only make Jack more determined. She poured the drinks without comment, omitting her own glass until Jack said, "Drink!" She did not argue. Sipping, she wondered if she might be sick . . . if Jack would let her off then.

Nico's thoughts were unfathomable. There was no guessing how much of this he understood or how much he was affected by the drink, or by the quite obvious foreplay in which Jack and Lotte were now engaged.

Marianna could not look at any of them. In one final heroic gulp she managed to finish her brandy and, after a moment's bracing, to stand up. "I'm going to bed," she announced. "I feel awful."

"So soon?" Jack was no longer sharply focused. He squinted at her, then at Nico. "On your feet, man."

If the words were incomprehensible, the upward snap of Jack's head was explicit enough. Nico emptied his glass and stood up.

"No, really," Marianna said.

"We wouldn't want anyone getting lost."

"I can find my way. And I won't try anything . . ."

"I know. We don't make the same mistake twice. You've got yourself a watchdog," as if he had read her mind. He shot a string of words at Nico, and this time it was Marianna who found them incomprehensible. Nico nodded grimly.

"Dovidjenja." Jack gave the word a nasty twist.

She could not walk in a normal way. Her legs were like rods, her knees locked. She was agonizingly conscious of Nico, so close behind her that they touched if she hesitated for a second. They took a strange route through the monastery, through the kitchen and up an unlit interior stairway. Nico's great fist closed over her arm. Her heart was throbbing so violently that he must feel it, and for an awful moment she wondered if he might interpret this as passion. She kept her face rigidly averted and in her mind sent off wordless pleas indiscriminately to God and to Paul.

At her room, the instant that Nico released her, she grabbed at the doorknob, opened the door and slammed it in his face. She stood with her back braced against it, gasping for breath. Expecting the pressure of the door forced against her, she instead heard a decisive click.

Nico had locked the door from the outside. She was locked in. Half sobbing, half giggling, she slid to the floor.

Chapter 10

Long after that first flood of relief, the trembling went on. Marianna remained huddled against the door, dissolved. Every muscle and nerve, even her bones, felt watery. She could not have stood up.

But her mind jittered on in the darkness, incoherently at first, like anyone babbling about a narrow escape. Her fear of Nico did not dissipate all at once, it had been too great, too absorbing; nor did she altogether trust this reprieve. He was still there, she was certain, on the other side of the door, with the key. He would have heard her hysterical outburst, and now probably he could hear her breathing: the deep, deliberate, shuddering breaths that at last were bringing her shakes under control. She thought that she heard him move or sigh, like a restless animal, and she crawled away from the door to the thin rug beside her bed and reached for the lamp.

The grudging light, like a false dawn, was hardly an improvement. Marianna felt that she had fought her way out of a nightmare only to find herself back in a dreadful reality. Waking up was worse, demanding much more strength, more courage than she could summon. She still had to get away, to warn Paul. She had to get out of here, now, not waste any more time, but . . .

A terrible lassitude held her inert. It was an effort to turn her wrist so that she could see her watch. Twelve more hours. No, less than that. In less than twelve hours Paul would keep his fatal appointment and it would be too late.

No. She rejected the thought, resentfully, and in an access of weakness closed her eyes, resting her head against the bed. It was too much, too much to expect of her. Anyway, it was impossible, hopeless, suicidal to try . . .

When she opened her eyes again, twelve precious minutes had gone by, and she had lost the argument with herself. Her eyes rose involuntarily from her wrist to the high window above the bed. When she struggled up, cautiously, distrusting her legs still, the window looked a hair lower. By swinging the foot of the cot around, lifting and pivoting it so that the legs barely scratched against the stone floor, she brought the high end of the metal frame into position directly below the window. Stopping then just long enough to change into sneakers and shuck off her jacket—any further hesitation, she knew, would undo her—she stepped onto the edge of the bed, up onto the metal rod, and sprang.

It was a near thing. Arms, elbows, fingernails, even her armpits scrabbling at the rough plaster, and her toes stubbed against the wall or flailing, kicking, she somehow wriggled up and across the wide sill, scraping her ribs and breasts.

Hanging there, winded, bruised, she would not let herself think about the next step . . . or the next. The cloister was totally dark. There was no guessing what she would drop onto—or how far down it was. The light in her room was a mistake, outlining the window, thickening the darkness beyond, but there was no going back.

She squirmed around, reversing her position so that her feet dangled outside. Seen from above the room offered an almost cozy security. She glanced at the locked door . . . and let go, let herself drop.

She landed only slightly jarred on what felt like broken paving. Weeds sprouted from the cracks, wet and unpleasant to the touch. Except for the misty aureole around her own window, the darkness was opaque as velvet. There was no distinction between the overhanging roof and the open sky.

Hands extended to fend off unseen obstacles, feet groping, she inched along under Lotte's window—or where she judged Lotte's window to be; distance was distorted.

And her balance was off. She was weaving from side to side. On her right she ran into the low wall which seemed to define the raised inner quadrangle, overgrown and dripping. Some prickly stalk, a rose or a briar, snagged her hand. Sucking the scratch, she realized how unprotected she was, how vulnerable . . . to

God knew what. She stopped and stood absolutely still, her hands close to her body as she imagined snakes crawling through the wet night, or startled toads. Or low bats. And in the water . . .

She could not go on, that was certain.

Nor stay here, trapped in the cloister, until Jack found her. He would enjoy that.

Her widely dilated eyes registered a faint sliver ahead, not of light so much as incomplete darkness. Drawn to it, terrified of what—or whom—she might find, she crept forward, scarcely breathing.

She had come upon the way out of the cloister, through a low archway, then a slight jog to another arch that led into the reception hall. There was no sound but the touch of her own rubber soles on the paving. If Nico remained on guard at her door, he would not see her if she hugged the wall and ducked around to the inner stairs that twisted down to the kitchen . . .

She had remembered the knife. It would be something, not much, but better than nothing.

Listening, straining to hear Jack or Lotte, she felt her way down the steps. There was no sign of either of them. An obscure bulb had been left burning in the kitchen, and their dishes undisturbed around the sink.

The dining room was dark, the terrace empty . . . and then she was out of the monastery, guessing at the path, stumbling over uneven rocks.

The quiet licking of the water guided her along the shore. It was slow going. Even here, well away from the building, she was terrified of being heard, of starting a rock slide, or falling clumsily. The wet rocks were slippery. She held the knife blade away from herself so tightly that her fingernails dug into her palm. Eyes straining against this dreadful blindness, she could not be sure if she actually saw a glimmer of light on the opposite shore, or not.

At the point that she judged to be nearest to the other shore she stopped and removed her shoes and tied the laces together. She would want them again. The jagged ground would be impossible barefoot.

It was while she was thinking this, wondering how best to carry her shoes while she swam, that she heard the voice: a man's. Jack's, she was sure, becoming louder and louder as she stood there. She dropped the shoes, clutched the knife and waded into the water.

Her wet clothing began to drag at her. She stripped off everything but her bra and panties and struck out for the far shore, cutting through the black water with a gliding, quiet sidestroke. The water was icy on her body, swished past her ear. She felt tingly and exultant; she had made it.

The knife was cumbersome palmed under her thumb. For a moment she considered dropping it. And then, in almost the same instant, the water was churning behind her in a crazy turbulence, almost as if she had created a mammoth wake. The lake that had been smooth, hardly ruffled by her passage, erupted all at once in a wild commotion.

And something, not a weed, caught at her feet . . . caught and slipped off and caught again and clamped itself firmly around her ankle. She was pulled back, dragged under . . . drowning, she knew.

That certainty gave her a desperate strength. She kicked and flailed, arched and flipped her body—like a fish, a great thrashing hooked fish—and sank the knife into something. Something tough, with a bone. She let go.

The convulsion did not subside all at once, but it changed. Marianna's foot slipped free. Aching for air, she kicked back and away from a sort of whirlpool that threatened to suck her back into the struggle that went on and on—the death struggle, she thought, of whatever she had sunk the knife into. Gagging, she kicked again and swam away, doing a flat-out overhand crawl this time, until she scraped up at last on the far shore. And then she just lay there gasping, her lungs exploding.

Her internal pounding blocked out everything else so that for some time she was unaware of any other motion or sound, anything outside her own body. She did not understand that someone else had splashed into the shallow water until he was leaning over her. He stood dripping on her and feeling for her, running his hands over her until he found her armpits, then dragged her onto dry land. He grunted something unintelligible as he put her down. Nico.

She lay still, playing dead. *Playing* . . . she *was* dead. And after all that she would be hauled back so that Jack could kill her again properly, his way. Prisoners weren't allowed to die on their own; they were always saved for the hangman. The unions were strict about who did what. A sort of sob escaped her.

Nico prodded her again and, apparently satisfied, pulled her up onto her feet. He was less decisive about his next move. The chin carry à la junior lifesaving, Marianna wondered, or would he drag her back to the monastery by her hair?

He held her lightly, steadied against his wet shirt. Waiting for Jack? There was no sign of him. The lake had gone back to its placid licking. Yet she had heard him. She had been certain of that, an eternity ago. And then she had swung the knife at something, into something . . .

"Where's Jack?"

Nico's hand covered her mouth. He was not rough, but he was definite; and when she squirmed, he moved both hands so that they met around her neck with a gentle pressure that said enough. He let go then, only touching her spine to indicate that she should start walking . . . but away from the water into the impenetrable woods.

How far, how long they crashed on through those woods was all part of the inky blur of that night. Literally crashed—Nico made no attempt to be quiet—and stumbled. Marianna's feet were flayed but there was no hope of stopping. Nico's arm would go around her, forcing her on, and she went, shivering, with tears running down her cheeks. They did reach some sort of road or path, sandy and pebbly and so narrow in places that

Nico would go ahead and drag her along after him. That was all she ever remembered about their progress, that and the cold—like black ice—and Nico's unfathomable silence.

The port or fishing village, whatever it was, she sensed rather than saw: a few dark, sleeping houses by a pier. Here among the mooring lines Nico moved sure as a cat, talking now in a useless Serbo-Croatian mutter.

Marianna responded in English. "The telephone. There must be a telephone here. I've got to call Belgrade. Teléfono? Telefón?"

He understood. Snatching her wrist, he pulled her down into one of the boats. A spate of words came at her—of anger or explanation, she never knew. One thing was clear: she was to stay exactly where he put her, up forward, beside the pilot's wheel. She stood there shivering violently while he fiddled with the boat.

And then the engine roared into life, and there was a glimmer of light from the instrument panel. Nico's shadowed face was turned toward her, scowling ferociously. He looked at her for several seconds in open disapproval, then unbuttoned his shirt and handed it to her. It was damp still, but warm.

"Thank you."

He was busy with the lines, casting off fore and aft, and they were moving, chugging out into the predawn darkness. Marianna held her watch close to one of the dials. It had stopped. Three o'clock? Four? She had no way of knowing. The walk had seemed eternal.

"Please . . ." She said it gently, encouraged by Nico's

new mildness. He seemed almost relaxed. "I've got to call Belgrade. It's urgent. It's a life-and-death matter, really, literally. I've got to reach Belgrade somehow. Belgrade," she repeated loudly as the one possible common denominator.

"Beograd!" He threw back his head with a great roar of laughter. "Beograd!" his hands sketching the fact that this was a boat and Beograd was not on the sea. It was inland, miles inland, and might just as well have been a million miles away, Marianna concluded. There was no way of stopping Paul. No way. The slang expression repeated itself, hammering at her. No way. No way to Belgrade.

"Dubrovnik?" she said.

"Korčula," Nico countered.

Chapter 11

Korčula. An island, then a town emerged from the first vague, colorless light like a mirage—a miracle of civilization; bunched houses and hotels, an excursion steamer. Marianna took back every critical thought she had ever had about tour groups and prayed to God that she would find one here. Even asleep the ancient town had a promising this-century air about it.

And across a narrow channel—she turned slowly, incredulous, superstitious, almost afraid to believe what she saw for fear that it would go away or Nico would read her mind; her reactions soared off in all directions —was the mainland. Or a painted backdrop of the mainland with massive, towering mountains and a thin horizontal band for the highway.

Nico was eyeing her doubtfully. His shirt hung to her knees, sleeves flopping over her wrists. She could well imagine how she looked, battered and bedraggled, in any event unlikely to want to go anywhere by daylight. He turned back to what he was doing, to bringing the boat neatly alongside.

Just before the first gentle bump, she was off. Running was excruciating—every cut on her feet protested —but she could not stop now. Pure desperation kept her going, feet slapping on the pier and the road while Nico secured the boat—a few seconds' head start. She did not look back.

The palm trees and hedges in front of the hotel took on color as she came near. She shot between them. There was no one about, to her intense relief; a night light beginning to fade in the lobby, no staff on duty yet, a telephone. She jiggled it prayerfully.

This time—another miracle—the operator confessed to a slight knowledge of English. Marianna enunciated distinctly. "The American Embassy. American, yes. In Belgrade."

"The American Embassy? In Belgrade?" There was a long clicking wait, then the operator again at last, sounding out each syllable maddeningly, twice. "The number for the American Embassy in Belgrade is six four five six five five. That is Belgrade six four five six five five. I will ring it."

More than the usual telephonic sounds intervened and then, an eternity later after prolonged ringing, a voice emerged as if from under water; there were bubbly echoes.

"The Ambassador, please! Yes, the Ambassador," Marianna repeated. "Mr. Boyd Currier."

"Madame, please. There is no one. At this hour. If

you will call back . . ."

"Then I'll call him at home. Give me the Ambassador's residence. Please. Don't hang up."

"I'm sorry, madame. If you will call back later . . ."

"No, *please,* you don't understand," Marianna began, but the line had gone dead.

Brightly colored brochures, a rack of them on the desk, mocked her. Brilliant blue skies and water, green islands, red and white villages, the perfect setting for a carefree vacation with all kinds of tours, all-inclusive, wonderfully well organized. The map on the wall showed a choice of islands strung along the Dalmatian coast—and Belgrade in the interior, deeply, hopelessly embedded behind the mountains.

There was a flicker of motion in the mirror beyond the map: a wild-eyed face and spiky, salt-matted hair; a demented-looking woman in a man's shirt. She would not have known herself.

Outside the morning light had come on quickly, and someone was walking along the far side of the hedge. She did not stop to see if it was Nico but, crouching, scuttled into the darker interior of the hotel. She held her breath, listening, and opened doors and peeped around them with the greatest caution. She felt furtive and hunted, exactly in fact like her own ghastly reflection. Anyone who saw her would assume the worst, would *know;* she was obviously guilty of something. Theft . . . or murder?

Angled passages had brought her into a big tiled

kitchen. Unlike Nico's, this one was tidy and scrubbed. There was no knife left to rust by the sink. But she suddenly felt one in her hand, going through flesh, up against bone . . .

No. She shook her head violently, fighting off the thought. She had only imagined that. Her fingers caught in her tangled hair. She had had no sleep, that was all, and no food.

Opening more doors, she found bread and oranges and in a storage cupboard, hanging on a nail, a limp blue garment, a sort of smock, almost a dress. At least it was slightly more presentable than Nico's shirt, if coarse and unpleasant against her skin.

More than anything at that moment—insanely, she thought, watching herself with an odd detachment— she longed for a bath and her own clean clothes. With no money, no passport, no time—perhaps some six hours left—she craved a hairbrush. It was as if she had accepted defeat. Convinced that she could not get through to Paul, she had settled for a possible goal. By prowling through the hotel, room after room, surely she would find a hairbrush. She really had flipped. She heard herself giggle.

Or someone had giggled, and now a rear door was opening. Marianna edged into the passageway and ran back the way she had come.

There was only one thing to do. Before she was dragged off to the police, looking guilty, she must go to them herself—for help. She glanced down doubtfully at her bloodstained feet. They would have to believe her. And do something. Do what? Arrest her? Or arrest Paul and shoot him at dawn for conspiring to blow up their Predsednik? Or . . . oh, God. She stopped absolutely still.

Chapter 12

It was probably close to six when the harbor came fully awake, early still, but the sun had risen some distance while the first fishermen puttered about with their lines and gear.

Marianna had watched them. Crouched behind a beached dory, she was pulled apart by indecision: whether to ask one of them to help her, to take her to the mainland—and in what language, what currency? Money might have been understood, but . . .

She huddled into the stolen smock. Any move would be conspicuous—and almost certainly futile. Yet . . .

The terrible urgency pulled at her physically, the minutes ticking by . . . a time bomb. Did letter bombs, she wondered, have timing devices?

The significance of the luggage did not penetrate her nightmare at first. It collected bit by bit, a lumpy valise and a pair of strapped baskets, then some good matched sets, leather and aluminum and canvas, until what had begun as a small cairn on the pier became a major and familiar outcropping, a sure sign of a tour group. The leader stood pointing and gesticulating, directing people now, his back to Marianna.

"Ivo!" She ran toward him, not feeling the stones under her bare feet, feeling nothing but relief—a tremendous surge of relief that propelled her toward him. She repeated his name as she ran and had almost reached him when he at last turned and she saw his face —his totally unfamiliar and, as he looked at her, appalled face. The beginning of an easy smile faded into wary concern.

Marianna was sobbing for breath. "I'm sorry. I thought you were Ivo. I . . . do you speak English?"

"Yes." Even this admission was guarded; and no wonder, she thought. She could imagine how she looked to him: awful. Crazy. Stark raving mad. The whole group was goggling at her as if she were one of the more sensational sights.

"Look. I know"—she threw out her hands, pleading —"but I'm all right. I mean, I need help. Please . . . are you going to the mainland?"

The group went into a mumbled conference, questioning each other. English was apparently not their language. Only the leader showed the slightest understanding and he was quiet for some time, working out what she had said.

"You know Ivo," he said cautiously. "You know he is coming here?"

"I was with his group and when I saw you, I thought . . . but you're right. I mean, no, we weren't coming here, not to any of the islands." She had lost him. She was saying too much, too fast, confusing him. There wasn't time for explanations anyway. "Look, I'll explain all that later, but right now it's an emergency."

He had looked away and was scowling at the water. "There," he said, pointing.

What had been a featureless white dot gradually became a motor launch with a white wake. It made a wide, semicircular approach that sent waves splashing against the pier.

And then it was bobbing alongside, and Ivo jumped ashore with a line in his hand. Ivo. She was hallucinating. No, it was Ivo. She was certain this time.

If he saw Marianna, he did not recognize her. When he had secured the boat, he exchanged some incomprehensible comments with his fellow tour guide—jokes, Marianna judged by the way they grinned at each other—before his attention was drawn to her.

"Remember me? Marianna Eames."

He looked perplexed, blank.

"I was with your tour. Until Split." The pun threatened to overwhelm her. A sobbing, insane laugh escaped.

And then Ivo put out both his hands and said, "My dear!" She threw her arms around him.

"My dear," he said again. "What happened?"

She did not release him altogether but held onto his hands as if they were a lifeline. "You've got to help me. Take me with you."

"Of course."

"To the mainland."

"Yes. All these people . . . they are going to join my tour. To go to Dubrovnik." He was studying her closely, talking in a jerky, distracted way. His doubts and discomfort were obvious, and the unasked questions. Along with his accent he seemed to have acquired a certain British reticence so that, dismayed as he might be by her appearance, he did not comment. He scanned the dock and said, "Of course," again, vaguely.

"Now? Right away? It's urgent. I'll explain."

He nodded solemnly. "Okay."

"But *hurry!*"

He grinned. With this and a few rapid, foreign words he brought on a burst of action. The two tour guides began to toss suitcases into the launch, then handed in their charges with a flourish, making a game of it, a race. The tour group, caught up in this new tempo, tumbled into seats in the stern and sat bouncing, urging the boat on. In high spirits they shouted encouragement to a trio of latecomers who came running across the pier: three men. The middle one, his big hands frantically flailing, broke away from the other two and raced ahead. It was Nico.

"Oh, God, hurry. Don't wait." Marianna dug her fingernails into Ivo's arm. "Please . . ."

"Okay, okay."

The other guide hopped ashore, laughing—it was still part of the game—and cast off the lines. The boat thrummed forward, separating itself from the land by a wider and wider milky froth.

The cheering and clapping crescendoed, then came

to a ragged end after someone murmured, "Policija?"
The word was passed around uneasily.

"If it's police . . . ?" Ivo said. His face was creased
again by worry, indecision.

"You can't go back. No matter what . . ."

Nico was shouting above the noise of the engine, but
his gestures alone were plain enough—and his rage, the
desperate rage of a doomed animal.

"He says . . ." Ivo could not manage these words.
Nothing in his training had prepared him for such a
moment. He stared agonized at Marianna for a moment, then tried again. "He says that you killed a man."

"Don't listen. Just go. I'll tell you on the way."

"But if it's true . . ."

"Go! There's no time now. I'll explain."

"The police. There will be bad trouble. I will be
blamed."

"If you don't hurry, someone else will be killed. Your
Predsednik . . ."

His expression warned her that she had gone too far
to be believed. His initial shock gave way to visible
relief, a faint comprehending smile.

"I know. I know how it sounds. Crazy, insane, you
think I'm making it up. But I'm not. There's an incredible plot, you've got to believe me, or it will be too late.
Don't listen to him . . ."

"A plot?" Ivo repeated the word, wavering, his troubled gaze moving back and forth between Nico's raging
and Marianna's pleading.

"I'll tell you while we go. It's too complicated."

"Then we must tell the police, if there's a plot."

"They won't believe me, don't you see! You didn't. And they've been listening to Nico."

He turned back to the controls, scowling, unsure. The other guide was shouting at him now from the shore. Marianna found that she was holding her breath, clenching her fists. She staggered backward as the boat lunged ahead at full speed.

The shots sounded almost immediately, warning shots, over their heads. The tour group ducked in unison and slid down onto the deck.

"They won't shoot us. They won't take a chance . . . on hitting innocent bystanders . . . will they?" Marianna's voice trailed away.

Ivo looked straight ahead, grimly. "I don't know. But they'll be waiting for us at Orebíc. The police will. They will have been called."

"Can't we land somewhere else?"

He shook his head mournfully and jerked his chin toward the other passengers. "The bus is there. The others are waiting . . ."

Another shot rang out.

"Whatever the trouble is," he went on, "you'd better tell me now, quickly. The crossing is very fast."

Hurried, with the land looming closer and closer, the story tumbled out: Paul and Boyd, Lotte, Jack, Nico, a jumble of details. To make him understand how everything had happened, step by step, Marianna put in too much. "You see, I had no choice, no money. After Paul disappeared, there I was, you can't imagine . . . and then when my passport was gone and my last cent. Of course I know now that they took my purse, Lotte and Jack. Even at the time I suspected them, but I couldn't be sure . . . and I wanted to believe them, about meeting Paul on that little island. They seemed to know all about Paul and Boyd and why Paul had to go off so suddenly. It was all very hush-hush."

Ivo shook his head in annoyance. "Never mind all that. Tell me about the plot. Exactly."

"I don't know."

"Don't know!" He turned on her, shocked and then murderous, choking. "You don't know!"

"Not exactly. All I know is . . ."

"You knew enough back there. Enough to run away from the police." The enormity of his own part overwhelmed him, and he spun the wheel recklessly, turning the boat sharply, as if to go back. "The Predsednik, you said. You said he was in danger and I believed!" he railed at himself, his voice cracking.

They had made a full turn. Marianna caught at the wheel and swung her whole body against it. The boat tilted, rocked, steadied itself as their opposed weights came into a straining balance.

"There's a bomb. I heard that much." Marianna shouted above Ivo's bitter tirade. They were both panting, struggling for control of the wheel. "A letter bomb. In the Ambassador's credentials. He's supposed to call on the Predsednik this morning. To present his credentials. But it will be Paul taking his brother's place. For security reasons, he thinks. He doesn't know about the bomb."

"He must be stopped!"

"I know."

"Arrested."

"No! We've got to stop him ourselves. If they find the bomb on him . . ."

"They'll kill him," Ivo said, "and ask questions later." There was approval in his attitude.

And he had relaxed his grip on the wheel so that now they were steering in the same direction, both urging the boat toward the mainland, but for quite different reasons.

Chapter 13

The dress fitted badly, sliding off her shoulders—one of those slippery packable materials with a smeary print and a faintly clammy feel. Marianna had pulled it out of the nearest suitcase, along with a scarf for her hair and a pair of slippers, to the astonishment of the owner. A heavy German-looking woman had started forward, her face blazing.

"Tell her it's all right. Tell her I'll give them back."

Ivo had snapped something—Marianna extracted only the word Predsednik—and the woman had subsided, glowering. There was another gasp from the stern when she pulled off the smock and threw it overboard and slipped the dress over her head. It was an improvement anyway; and with her hair and feet covered, she had some hope of looking respectable, credible.

"Ivo, listen. Paul doesn't know about the bomb. He's innocent."

"As long as he's stopped . . ."

"But they'd be shooting the wrong person."

He shrugged, staring ahead with ferocious concentration. He looked very young—and terrified. They were almost in.

"Let me try to stop him. My way. Through the Embassy."

The landing took all his attention. He slowed the boat, bringing it alongside, and cut the engine.

"We'll try everything. But the Embassy first, then the police." Her voice was suddenly much too loud. There was nothing to shout above but the wash of water against the pier . . . and, now, squealing around the turn onto the long stone jetty, a small car.

"As I told you," Ivo said, "the police." He was resigned, watching the two men slam out of the car, and when they arrived at the edge of the pier, he tossed them a mooring line with an air of surrender.

Then everyone was talking at once in assorted languages. Understanding none of them, Marianna could only guess that the German woman was demanding her dress while the police, ignoring her, rasped at Ivo, whose voice was barely audible in the general discord.

It was one of the policemen who at last achieved a muttering sort of silence and having gained command ordered everyone out of the boat. Scowling and obviously dissatisfied, he watched closely as they scrambled onto the pier, one by one, then jumped into the boat himself and pushed among the luggage and opened the lockers. Frustration fed his anger. He was beside himself when he again shouted at Ivo.

Ivo pointed to something in the water. Standing next

to him on the pier, Marianna could not be sure if she saw or imagined the blue smock on the surface. In any case both the policemen were infuriated by whatever Ivo was saying. Infuriated and scornful: the one on the pier spat derisively into the water, then jumped aboard. The boat rocked and roared into action and Ivo, looking stunned, cast off the line.

"I don't get it," Marianna said as soon as she could make herself heard. The boat had made a tight, angry turn that sent a double wash back against the pier. Nor apparently did anyone else quite understand what had happened. Having watched the boat swerve off, the tour group turned their round-eyed, suspicious attention to Ivo.

"Hurry!" was all he said in a dazed tone.

"What . . . ?"

"Later." He started off with a wide swing of his arm but did not look back to see if the group was obediently following. They were in fact mutinous: they wanted their luggage. Ivo did not so much as break stride. His face was set, awed, Marianna thought. She had trouble keeping up with him—the borrowed slippers flapped off when she tried to run—and she eyed the police car longingly. "Ivo, look . . ."

"No! It's bad enough . . . The bus."

The tour group swarmed after him like enraged hounds. There was a nasty tearing sound as one of them caught at his shirt and he wrenched free. The water-front blurred by. Marianna saw nothing but Ivo pounding ahead—it would have been hard to say whether he was the pack's leader or its quarry—and then incredibly, when her lungs threatened to burst, there was the tour bus, the familiar fat green-windowed bus. Not only there but throbbing and foul, polluting the air, ready to go.

Marianna fell into a seat.

"Well!"

She was too exhausted to respond. Her pounding ears shut out everything else for some time—everything but the blessed grinding of the gears as the bus heaved into jolting motion.

Ivo clung to a rail next to the driver like a prize fighter on the ropes. The German tourists were not appeased. Jounced and thrown by the speeding bus, they continued to harangue at Ivo until he drew himself up—heroically, Marianna thought—and drawing on some last reserve of strength snapped an order. He pointed a straight finger at some empty seats.

The woman next to her raised her voice. "So you changed your mind. Decided to come with us after all." It was Miss Hawthrone, triumphantly. She had hitched herself around to inspect Marianna. "I wouldn't have known you. I didn't at first when you came running up. We all wondered what was taking so long. They'd kept us waiting long enough, after getting us up with the birds and hurrying us through our breakfast. Hurry up to wait."

Miss Hawthorne's complaints were perfunctory, however. She was far more interested in Marianna's appearance. "I see your boy friend isn't with you," she said slyly.

Marianna said nothing. Mr. Whitcomb, she saw now, was hanging over the back of the seat. His welcome, like Miss Hawthorne's, was vindictive. "His loss," he said happily, "is our gain. Didn't quite live up to expectations, eh?"

"These things happen, I imagine. These brief encounters." Miss Hawthorne giggled. "One never knows. But how could one . . . on such short acquaintance? I mean, whether the man was all he seemed. He might be handsome, I grant you, but . . ."

But not to be trusted, she meant. Not to be counted on or believed. He might turn sour at any moment and leave you.

Miss Hawthorne pressed forward with her hints like a monstrous quizmaster bent on extracting the answers. "It must've been pretty bad," she concluded, "if you can't even talk about it. And judging by the state you're in . . . Well, what did happen?"

Marianna drew a deep breath. "He had to take a bomb to the President."

Miss Hawthorne recoiled. Mr. Whitcomb, after a doubtful instant, pounded the back of the seat and laughed. "A bomb, you said? To the President? That's a good one. I always said Mrs. Eames was a great little kidder. Should have come up to Mostar with us, with an imagination like that . . . yeah."

"Well!" Miss Hawthorne was purple with offense. "She didn't have to be rude."

The bus jolted and swayed. Marianna staggered up the aisle and, steadying herself, caught at people by mistake—a shoulder, a head, someone's hair. Ivo stood with his feet braced wide, less punchy now but still gripping the rail by the driver. Watching Marianna's drunken progress, he managed a tired smile. His eyes were bloodshot. "My dear," he said.

"They didn't believe me," she began. "About Paul."

"No." He paused to marshal the words. "I told the police at Orebić what you said also. They did not believe me. They thought it was a . . . a crazy story, I don't know." He looked lost; his English, too, seemed to have abandoned him. "A diversion?"

"A red herring?"

He shrugged, still perplexed. "I don't know. They did not want to hear about it, whatever it was. This change of subject, do you say? They only cared about finding the American woman. In the blue smock. They had been called from Korčula that I was bringing her to the mainland. She had killed a man. They had their orders. I tried to tell them . . . what you said . . . about the bomb, the Predsednik. They called me names. They said I was a fool, a crazy, a stupid to listen to you. They said you had told a story to take away my attention, so that you could get away. They said the American woman had made a fool of me and I should be shot. They said . . ."

He was more and more incensed, reliving that moment. Marianna remembered the angry scene, the furious search by the police and their scathing treatment of Ivo. He had been humiliated and badly frightened . . . and proud.

As if he had read her thoughts, his face began to clear. The troubled look was replaced by a widening grin. "Stupid," he repeated, "to let you jump overboard, not to go back for you." Ivo looked extremely young and naughty at that moment, his eyes brimming with mischief.

Marianna started to laugh. "You didn't try to save me? I might have drowned!"

"They went back for you. They could see your blue smock in the water, when I pointed to it."

If she had thrown her arms around him right then, they both would have been thrown off balance. The jouncing bus required a tight grip. She could only smile at him gratefully.

"They should not have called me those names," he said, and then, fervently, raising his eyes to the roof of the bus, "but there had better be a bomb now. It had better be real, and we had better do something about it fast. Or else . . ." He looked at her wanly and added, "My dear," with the gentlest irony.

Or else. Marianna winced. It was no longer the least bit funny. Ivo had defied the police. The consequences were unthinkable. She caught at his wrist, twisting his watch around.

Ivo ducked to look out the window. "There should be a telephone soon, when we get to the highway."

"Someone must be at the Embassy by now. They've got to be." Got to be, got to be, please. Marianna sent up another formless prayer.

The bus pitched and ground its way along the mountainside. Standing there swaying—unwilling to leave Ivo's side although they avoided each other's eyes—Marianna could see only the sheer drops and dizzy rises of land at the edge of the road, tinted by the green glass.

There were conventional squeals from the back of the bus now and then, but the group had survived many similar roads by now. Even the bridge foursome showed a certain matched aplomb. They were paired off exactly as they had been before, always: the bridge players and the gays across from the middle-aged married couples, the mother and son opposite the honeymooners; except that Mr. Whitcomb was in process of attaching himself to Miss Hawthorne, as if Marianna's shocking behavior had brought them together.

The remarkable aspect was that so little had changed. Marianna felt that she had been away from them for weeks. Pursuing this thought aloud, she told Ivo, "I didn't expect to catch up with you so soon. I thought you'd gone on to Dubrovnik at least, or farther. Thank God you hadn't."

"Ah, Dubrovnik," he sighed. All Yugoslavs seemed to speak of Dubrovnik with wistful pride, but Ivo expressed a much deeper longing. If he had been in Dubrovnik, he would not be here—in the worst possible trouble. "You have forgotten our itinerary," he said sadly. "Mostar, Orebíc. *Then* Dubrovnik. Now. Next."

This time he was the one to twist his wrist around. "In an hour, a little more."

It was almost half past eight. Only two and a half more hours. In two and a half hours, unless she could stop him . . . Paul.

The bus swerved off the road. Marianna clutched and caught herself. Lost in her private worries, she had not been paying attention. She was trembling as they came to a sudden, silent stop.

"Now what?" came Miss Hawthorne's scolding voice. "Why is he stopping? Haven't we had enough delays?"

"The telephone," Ivo told Marianna. For all the good it would do, he implied.

Chapter 14

"Belgrade, six, four, five, six, five, five."

Marianna paid out the numbers with the utmost care, like bets, as if she were risking her last chips. Which, in a sense, she was. This was her last hope: all or nothing, life or death. "Six, four, five, six, five, five," she confirmed as Ivo translated the numbers to the operator.

He looked pale in the dim hallway and shaken. They had come into some sort of inn or café—Marianna had noticed very little about the place. Kitchen sounds came from somewhere behind the yellowed plaster wall, and a hint of drains.

Ivo drummed and fidgeted. Faced with reporting a highly improbable bomb story to the police, again— and this time at a really formidable level in the capital —he seemed to have developed a bad case of stage fright. The call to the Embassy, he conceded, should be put through first.

"*Halo...dobro...* yes, please wait a minute," he said then in English and handed the telephone to Marianna.

"Hello . . ."

The answering voice was wide-awake, cordial, not the night switchboard operator. Marianna heard it with a rush of relief. "I've got to talk to the Ambassador," she said. "It's an emergency."

"The Ambassador?" There was the faintest shading of withdrawal. "If you're in trouble, perhaps someone else . . ."

"No."

"Perhaps I could help you, if I knew what sort of trouble."

"I've got to talk to *him.* Right away." Marianna took a deep breath, fighting to stay calm, to sound confident, to keep the quaver out of her voice. "Or his brother. Is Paul Currier there?"

This was a mistake. The voice retreated farther. "There is no one by that name that I know of. I'll connect you with the Ambassador's secretary. Just a minute, please. Hold on."

A minute, another delay, another voice: this one forbidding from the start, as if her proximity to the Ambassador made her his last hope in a long line of crumbling defenses. This one, like a good sentry, would admit no one until his identity had been not only established but proved beyond reasonable doubt, and she clearly found Marianna's responses irregular.

"A friend of the Ambassador, you said. If it's a personal call, Mrs. Eames," she went on, voicing her dissatisfaction, "perhaps we could call you back this afternoon."

"I'm not a friend of his. I mean, I'm a friend of his brother's. It's about his brother, but . . ."

"Oh. Well then"—the secretary was audibly relieved; the Ambassador's brother was not her responsibility—"it will just have to wait."

But it couldn't wait, it couldn't, Marianna wanted to scream. She fought for control. Screaming would be the worst thing.

"This morning, you see," the implacable voice continued, "the Ambassador will not be in his office. He has an extremely important appointment. He will go directly."

"I know. He's going to present his credentials to the President. At eleven o'clock."

The secretary's stammer was confirmation enough. So Jack had been telling the truth.

"That's the point. We've got to warn him. Quickly! They're going to stop him somehow. They're sending his brother instead."

"They? Who?"

"I don't know. But they're going to plant a bomb. A letter bomb," Marianna specified, hearing herself—hearing her wild accusations as they must sound to the Ambassador's secretary: unbelievable, unsubstantiated, becoming shrill. "A bomb among his credentials!"

"Is this a prank . . . or a threat? Because if it is," the secretary went on icily, "you can expect the gravest consequences. The proper authorities will be informed, I assure you . . . not only the Ambassador, but the police."

"Yes. Fine. That's what I wanted to do. Tell them . . . I don't know exactly, but somehow Paul's being made to take his brother's place. He thinks he's saving his life. I don't know what they're going to do to the Ambassador, maybe kidnap him. But you've got to understand. Paul is innocent. He doesn't know about the bomb. You mustn't let them . . ."

Shoot him? Marianna couldn't say it. She felt that she had turned Paul in, condemned him.

"Kidnap . . . the Ambassador?"

"If I could just talk to him," Marianna pleaded. "Is he at the residence?"

"I will see that he gets your message, personally, I promise you, Mrs. Eames. If he should want to call you back . . ."

"I won't be here. I'll be on the bus to Dubrovnik."

"Where are you calling from?"

"From . . ." Marianna searched the dim yellow hallway. Ivo was not there. "I don't know," she confessed.

"You don't know? Oh. I see."

Ivo, when Marianna found him, was pacifying the tourists. He raised his eyebrows, looking wretched.

"Done," she told him cautiously. "At least I tried. I told her everything I could, for all the good it did. I don't think she believed a word of it. Bitch!"

Faces swiveled in her direction: shocked, curious, primarily hostile. Marianna lowered her voice. "I don't know that I blame her. It did sound fantastic. Bombs, kidnapping. I must have sounded like some wild-eyed

147

crank raving on. And to top it off I didn't know where I was. I couldn't tell her where I was calling from, which really did sound insane, or criminal—or both. It was all she needed."

Ivo edged around her toward the door of the bus. "If you're worried about calling the police," Marianna said, "don't bother. She assured me that she would. With 'gravest consequences,' she said."

Ivo looked sick.

"We can't just sit here. Waiting to be caught," Marianna added, thinking suddenly of sheep and goats and how you might as well be hung for one as the other, an old saying which she spared Ivo. "As long as we're in this far, up to our necks, we've got to do everything we can . . . at least *try* to clear ourselves. And Paul."

Ivo hesitated on the step.

"How far is Belgrade?" she said.

"Too far."

"But flying . . . from Dubrovnik? How far is the airport?"

He shrugged. "An hour? Then the plane. The flight is maybe two hours, and it leaves at nine o'clock, so you see . . ."

"If we hurried. We could try at least. We're wasting time here. Let's go!"

There was a mumble of approval from the tour group. "And about time," Miss Hawthorne said. "Really!"

*　　　*　　　*

The bus took off all at once, shuddering and growling, Marianna thought, like some great clumsy animal flogged into motion.

"You'd better sit down. And hang on," Ivo warned. He sounded grim and angry, snapping orders at the driver, and when he slipped into the seat next to her, he did not look at Marianna but straight ahead, tight-faced. There was a suggestion of revenge; she had asked for this.

The spectacular vistas of the Adriatic highway spun past, green precipices plunging into turquoise sea. Marianna's stomach seemed to flop over. But not looking, closing her eyes, she was all the more sickened by the hurtling motion.

A sure sense of disaster overwhelmed her. She had asked for it, she thought again. Insisted, stubbornly. It was her decision that they must go . . . *now.* That they must hurry, race against time, against all the odds, no matter what anyone else said. She had decided, no matter what.

The brakes grabbed in panic. Her whole body clutched . . . for the inevitable skid . . . the sprung door. It was happening again. For an instant she saw Ted lying in the road. She had been in such a hurry. And now . . . again.

She opened her eyes. The bus had swayed back into its lane, and the voice was Miss Hawthorne's, complaining. "You could at least tell us where we are, young man."

"Or where we've been," Mr. Whitcomb said from behind a jiggly map, "since it's impossible to read under these conditions."

"I thought we were going to stop at Ston," someone wailed. It was one of the gay couple. "And Trsteno, where Byron visited. You promised."

"I'd so looked forward to the botanical gardens," the dropout's mother said. "I read about herbal cures all the time." She laughed lightly at herself. "Tansy, you know, even in the Middle Ages . . ."

"She's always looking for a miracle," her son muttered, and it was hard to tell whom he was accusing.

Ivo's expression remained stony, resistant. Marianna could almost feel the effort he was making not to respond, not to explode and tell them all to go to hell. He had been a good guide, patient and knowledgeable. Now . . .

He glared at her as if he knew what she was thinking. He would lose his job at the very least. He would probably go to jail. Or worse.

There was nothing that she could say. Ted's death had been her fault. Would there be others? Paul? Ivo? She turned away and stared through the tinted window at the blurred view.

The tour group, on the other hand, still had plenty to say. The price of the tour had included the services of a guide—and a competent driver. This careening race, bypassing the sights . . . well! Nor did Ivo's silence help. He sank lower in his seat.

"Why don't you tell them?" Marianna said.

"Tell them what?" he said without turning, defeated.

"Tell them it's all my fault, I insisted, I've got to get to the airport. Tell them why. We're trying to save a life, lives . . ."

He seemed to find a certain gallows humor in this. "The airport is not on the itinerary. And you . . ."

"Oh, I know. I've caused enough trouble," Marianna flared up. "And I'm not even on this tour. I left it. I suppose they resented that, too."

Ivo shrugged. "They talked about you, yes."

"And I'm sure they thought I deserved whatever happened." She looked down at herself wryly, remembering the ugly dress and flapping slippers. "They should be pleased."

They sounded anything but pleased, however. The bridge foursome raised its voices now, not quite in unison. "But that looks like Dubrovnik. It is; I'm sure it is. We should have turned. Back there. Ivo!"

He stood up, saying, "Ladies, please . . ." helplessly, and sat down again.

Mr. Whitcomb had started to shout, "Stop the bus! I demand that you stop this bus this instant. I will not be cheated out of Dubrovnik. I'll demand my money back."

Miss Hawthorne said very much the same thing, and several others took up the chant, ineffectually. Their protests weakened gradually as Dubrovnik receded— or perhaps it was just that they now faced the other

151

way, looking back. As the bus climbed inexorably away
from it, they had a stunning view of the entire walled
city reduced to toy size.

Ivo did not look back. He had slumped onto the very
base of his spine in a despondent fold.

"I'm sorry. I know how you feel." Marianna wanted
to take his hand, but he was in no mood for comfort. He
had made a hostile wall of his misery. "It will all work
out . . . somehow," she said without conviction.

Ivo snorted. "By a miracle? The police will give me
a reward for helping you to escape? Maybe it will work
out for you."

"Ivo, if I did kill Jack . . ."

"What I need," he said, ignoring her, "is the plane to
Rome—or London—not Belgrade."

"But you can't run away. That would be the worst
thing to do. And you've got to help me. Ivo . . ."

He looked at her coldly.

The airport was on a high plateau at the top of a
suddenly flat world, so that the runways ended in space.
Marianna noticed this and the plane drawn up to the
modern terminal with a small fraction of her mind. The
rest, now that they were here, was engulfed in panic.

"Ivo," she repeated. "Please. I don't speak the language. I don't have any money. I know, I should have
thought of that before, but . . ."

He had pulled himself out of the seat and stood with
his back to her, slightly hunched to watch their ap-

proach to the terminal. The driver parked the bus and cut the engine, but did not open the door. He turned, questioning, waiting for orders.

Mr. Whitcomb's voice was strident above the other muttering. He was outraged, he demanded an explanation, he held Ivo personally responsible. "And I warn you, young man, I will see to it that your behavior is reported to the highest authorities. The highest. I will see to that myself. And your job won't be worth that, not *that*." He snapped his fingers, sniffing. "It's criminal, that's what it is, carting us out here against our will. Criminal," he repeated in a lowered voice, as if aware for the first time that there was no need to shout. The bus was absolutely quiet.

So quiet that Miss Hawthorne's breathy little interjection was distinct. "We've been hijacked!" she said.

She was serious. Marianna turned to see her face, the high flush and wide, frightened eyes. The odd hush continued for several seconds. The bus felt sealed, claustrophobic, and the air heavy as if filled with explosive fumes.

Marianna did not remember jumping up. She was on her feet, facing the tour group. "She's right. Miss Hawthorne is right," she said, "but it's okay. There's nothing to worry about. Just hand over your money— your cash, dinars, that's all I want—and you'll be driven back to town. You can go on with your tour. Just your dinars," she repeated, moving to the back of the bus, "fast."

"Or else?" the college boy started bravely, but his throat seemed to close.

"Or the whole bus blows sky-high. Ivo will see to that. *We* have nothing to lose."

She heard herself with a lightheaded sort of detachment. The voice was her own, but she had no idea where the extraordinary words came from. She was acting a part, in costume. The dress kept falling off her shoulders and the slippers were too big. "Watch them, Ivo. If anyone tries anything . . ."

The hat came from the head of one of the bridge ladies, packable white cotton of a crew hat variety. Marianna held it by its brim as she backed slowly down the aisle and, marveling, watched it fill with bunched-up bills. She said, "Thank you," once and felt that it was inappropriate, like thanking people individually for their offerings in church. This, too, was impersonal, in a good cause.

Ivo was standing at the front of the bus. She could not look at him—hysterical laughter was building up, threatening to erupt—until she backed into him. "Okay. Now tell the driver, as soon as we're off, to drive them back to town.

"Tell him," she said with slightly less assurance, "to find them a new guide." She pushed the hat at him. "What you've got to do is talk us onto that plane. Come on."

Chapter 15

Straight off the end of the runway and they were airborne, banking. Beyond the window there was a tilted green and gray landscape and a blue slice of sea. Ivo saw none it. He looked straight ahead with a catatonic stare.

"You did it!" Marianna whispered. Her own reaction still tended toward hysteria, the pent-up giggles rising to the surface. "What on earth did you tell them?"

"Does it matter?"

She felt that he could not bear the sight of her. She had gone too far: hijacking, stealing, deliberately involving him. This on top of everything else. Whatever slim hope he might have had of exonerating himself was now destroyed.

"Might as well be hanged for a sheep as a goat." She touched his sleeve and he shook her off, glaring at her with the gravest distrust. "I mean, if you're in the soup anyway, what difference does it make? What if you do go in a little deeper?"

"It's not funny," he said.

"I know. But I had to have money. I didn't stand a chance otherwise. And you were terrific. What did you say?"

His look was scathing. "I said you had a nervous breakdown. You had been robbed in my country . . . your passport, your clothing, everything. It was for us to help you—a matter of pride, I told them—to escort you to your Embassy. They would be recompensed. I told all those lies." He dropped his head onto his hands.

"But it will be worth it, if we can stop Paul. There's still a chance."

"No." He rocked his head slowly back and forth, then raised it enough to look at his watch. "There is no chance. At eleven o'clock we will only be at the airport, if we are on time. No chance at all."

They found very little more to say after that. Once Marianna mentioned that she would like coffee. Ivo nodded toward the stewardess. "Tell her," he said.

"We ought to be planning . . . deciding what we're going to do when we get to Belgrade."

He made a bitter little sound.

"Where will the Predsednik be?" Marianna said.

"The Palace."

"If we went straight there . . . ?"

"It will be too late, remember? When we arrive, and then more than half an hour from the airport . . ."

"The bomb might not have gone off . . ."

"And they will let us run into the Palace, ha!" He gave her another scathing appraisal. "Do what you like. I am not the tour guide any more, remember?"

The mountains bristled below them, jagged, forbidding. A plane making an emergency landing would be impaled. Marianna rested her forehead against the vibrating window, watching the land slide by—a brooding, harsh, impenetrable land.

Ivo had put his head back and closed his eyes. It was a quarter to ten when Marianna first reached for his watch, then seventeen past, then ten of eleven and they were coming down into the great flat plain of the Danube.

The beautiful blue Danube: elegantly dressed couples waltzing, gliding, everything smoothed. This inappropriate picture flashed through Marianna's mind—when Paul was down there somewhere, she thought, on his way at this very moment, not knowing . . .

She saw him clearly for an instant before the unbearable image seemed to explode in her mind.

She clutched Ivo's arm. "You will go with me?"

He sat there as if he were dead until the plane bumped down, twice, and, roaring, cut its speed to taxi into the Belgrade airport.

Chapter 16

Donkey carts and farm equipment lumbered along the highway. Again and again their taxi was forced to a crawl, then would screech past in a burst of irritation.

Oblivious to the sights, Marianna found herself gazing at the back of the driver's head, gauging his temper. A peevish type, she decided, he would not react kindly if they could not pay the fare. He had already expressed himself—but mildly, with a long squint—when Ivo gave him their destination. It was, she supposed, a little like someone at Dulles Airport demanding to be taken to the White House on the double—someone seedy-looking, shabby and ill-kempt and not at all fit to associate with the President.

Miles of modest workers' houses ringed the rebuilt city. Tidy modern buildings, a river, a park: Marianna had only the haziest impression of the approach to the Palace. They were on a broad tree-lined boulevard, and then the cab stopped and the driver turned expressively. They had arrived and he expected his fare.

"Wait!" The word came out with a rasp, with authority, not her normal voice at all. "We're going to wait
right here until we find out what happened. Tell him
to park and . . ."

"And then?" Ivo said. It was a cruel question, unanswerable.

"Tell him," she said.

Ivo translated in a weary tone as if he had given up
long ago; things could hardly get worse. The driver was
less philosophical. The back of his neck was tinged an
ominous purple as he pulled into a parking place and
stopped the motor.

It was nearly noon. Turning his wrist to read his
watch, Marianna could feel Ivo's tension, the tightly
held fear. "The President's Palace," he murmured on
an awed note of discovery.

Whatever Marianna had feared, the scene looked
tranquil enough now. There were no gaping holes, nor
gaping crowds, no sirens or flashing lights. So far as she
could see the building looked solid, tranquil. The mid-
day traffic moved past freely.

The long black limousine detached itself from the
stream of cars before she fully understood its significance. And then her reflexes were all wrong. She
couldn't move, and the door wouldn't open; she was
yanking at the wrong handle.

Out of the cab at last, she stumbled over her own
slipper and kicked it away so that she was half barefoot
running after the limousine. When it slowed to turn

into the Palace, she caught at a rear door handle and held on, limping and dragged along beside it.

The interior was murky. She had seen only that there were heads in the back and now as she shouted Paul's name a face turned toward her behind the glass.

"Paul?" she said again. "Ambassador Currier?" Her voice trailed off. The face was not quite right, not quite as she remembered Paul, similar, but . . .

The car had stopped. Shouts came at her and someone was trying to break her hold on the door handle.

The man in the limousine was frowning, puzzled. He showed no sign of recognition, annoyance rather at being delayed by a distasteful scene. He rolled down the window—over the protests of his companion—just enough to speak to her. *"Gospodja, molim."*

"I'm sorry. I thought you were someone else. I thought you were American."

He looked at her closely, hearing her voice and seeing her more clearly without the glass. "Marianna?" he said cautiously. "I don't believe it. For God's sake . . . !"

He was groping, startled, not pleased. ". . . what in hell are you doing here?"

He was properly dressed for the occasion, rather forbiddingly formal, and his hair was changed, combed differently and the sideburns trimmed. But the change went much deeper. What chilled Marianna was his attitude, the tightly checked anger behind the deep scowl lines and rigid jaw. He was glowering at her as if *she* didn't understand that he was on an important mission, that this was hardly the time . . .

"There's a bomb," she said quietly. "Among your papers. A letter bomb."

"A bomb? No." If he was disconcerted, it was only for an instant. "No. You're wrong. Not in this car." He smiled very faintly. "Sorry, but I'm late already. We were delayed. So if you'll let go of the car. Please," he added with an odd intensity and a flick of his head and eyes toward the man in the seat beside him.

"You've got to believe me. Get rid of it! If you take it in there . . ."

The other man stiffened and spoke sharply to the driver.

"Get away, Marianna. Quickly. For God's sake." He spoke like someone in pain, or—she understood at last —someone with a gun jabbed into his ribs.

The car was moving again. And Ivo was behind it, on the other side. She had no memory of calling him, but there he was, reaching for that door.

The rest was blurred, happening all at once: the momentary distraction of the opening door, the jerking around, and the gun hand twisted so that the startled driver, looking back, found himself staring into the barrel of a small revolver. It was Paul who kept the gunman's right wrist clamped between his two hands, Ivo on the other side securing the man's other arm, bending it back until his grip slackened.

"Get in," Paul ordered her, and she had barely scrambled into the front seat when the car lurched backward, then shot ahead in a wide screeching turn away from the President's Palace.

161

"The bomb," she whispered.

Paul was giving the driver rapid, unintelligible orders.

"If we don't stop bouncing it around . . ." She tried to make herself heard.

Now Ivo was outshouting Paul in what sounded like desperate fury.

"Where is it?" She knelt on the front seat, facing them, ignored while the argument raged. They were no longer shouting at the driver, but at each other. On the floor, braced between Paul's feet, was a slim leather attaché case.

Marianna leaned over the back of the seat, reaching for it. "We've got to get rid of it . . . fast! Don't you see!"

"That's what I told him. The damned fool!" Paul was winded and his hand, the one holding the gun, shook with strain. "The river . . . off one of the bridges . . . would do the least damage. But he insists . . ."

"Give it to me." Stretching, she reached the handle of the case.

The driver meantime was coming to a confused stop at an intersection.

"No! Please," Ivo said in a strangled voice. His English seemed to abandon him. His face worked in helpless silence for a moment and then he repeated, "Please. The police."

"That's what he's been fussing about. He says it's his only defense," Paul explained. "If there's a bomb in my briefcase, it's the only evidence that there really was a plot against the Predsednik. Otherwise . . ."

Marianna slowly drew back her hand, looking at the case with new horror. "He's right, you know. Otherwise, without that, he'll never be able to clear himself with the police, ever. They'll want all kinds of proof, considering what he's done. For me," she added, as the seriousness of Ivo's situation again overwhelmed her. "We've got to help him now."

"Have we?" Paul's eyebrows rose in grim amusement. Gripping the gun, keeping it aimed at the man in the middle while he steadied the case between his feet, he clearly had all that he could manage.

And now they were being attacked from behind—by irate drivers, the absurdly everyday sound of horns and profanity.

Marianna spoke rapidly, lightly, slurring the facts. "I'd never have made it without him. There's a rumor around that I killed a man. Jack Dance. He pretended to be your friend."

Paul shook his head. The name meant nothing to him, but the man beside him reacted to it noticeably, with rancor. For a moment Marianna felt sick, carried back into that nightmare of blind swimming, of unseen hands clutching her in the thrashing black water.

"I would have been arrested for murder," she said, "but Ivo helped me get away so that I could try to stop you, to warn you about the bomb. I'd overheard Jack telling Lotte, but I couldn't reach you, I couldn't telephone . . ."

She stopped herself; there was no time for the whole story. "We've got to go to the police, for Ivo's sake."

Paul gave the order and the limousine moved ahead —at a stately tempo, like the lead car in a funeral cortege. The attaché case assumed the exaggerated importance of a casket.

It was necessary to talk, a nervous requirement to counteract the tension, although there was no doubt as to where everyone's thoughts were focused.

"I don't suppose I should squeeze this thing too tightly." Paul was absorbed in the pressure of his legs against the leather sides of the case. "I'm not sure how much it takes to set one of these babies off."

"Jack said they were unreliable. But it didn't matter one bit—politically," Marianna said in a brittle, unnatural voice. "The result would be the same whether you blew off your own head or the Predsednik's. Just so it was known that the American Ambassador was responsible for a bomb in the Palace, the damage would be done. So much for diplomatic relations with the United States . . ."

She could not take her eyes off the attaché case, the rich brown leather and elegant brass catches. It was probably Italian, she thought, admiring the fine stitches. But what held her morbidly fascinated was its secretive interior. Inside—and she had a superstitious feeling that if she looked away for an instant, it would go off—waited the slim little bomb.

"He should be a hero. Ivo should," she murmured. "They should give him a medal for saving the President's life. And yours."

"Just so he's not a dead hero," said Paul uneasily.

"Just so there is a bomb," Ivo corrected him with an effort, his voice cracking.

At this Marianna did look up. "What do you mean?"

"I mean that they would not think that I was a hero if there was not a bomb, if it was a . . ."

"A hoax," Paul supplied and Ivo nodded, gray-faced.

"So, either way, it doesn't help," Marianna said after a minute. She had gone back to contemplating the secretive case, no longer thinking that it might explode at any moment but imagining it as innocent, harmless. She had believed what she overheard, everything that Jack had said—Jack of all people! It had all started there, and she had dragged Ivo into it. "If there's a bomb in there, or not. Either way," she said, "it could be a disaster."

Until now she had hardly been aware of the chauffeur. Not so much driving as easing the car along, he had become timid and elderly, hands gripping the wheel, eyes darting. He scarcely moved his lips when he spoke.

"He says there's a car behind us," Paul translated. "Obviously following, at this speed. Anyone else would have passed us. Had you noticed?"

Marianna had not, but she saw it now: a taxi, *their* taxi, tagging along like a persistent sibling. "We didn't pay him. We told him to wait. I guess he wants his fare!"

It was ludicrous, so marvelously impertinent in the

circumstances, it was desperately funny. "Poor man. What a shock for him if we blow up in his face. Right in front of him, without paying!"

No one else laughed. It was as if the slightest vibration might be too much.

Chapter 17

"That last mile or so . . . unbelievable," Marianna said. And it did seem unreal already, here in the stodgy safety of the Ambassador's office.

She had been savoring the State Department seal, the familiar eagle, and the flag that she had always taken for granted. The old-fashioned building, like a solid hotel gone frumpy in its later years, was an unlikely bit of homeland, but this room with its signed, smiling photograph of the American President was wonderfully reassuring.

"I don't think any of us breathed."

"Georgy least of all." Paul laughed. He had hitched himself onto a corner of the big square desk where his brother sat. "I didn't really believe in your bomb," Paul admitted, "until I saw how Georgy was squirming. He knew it was for real. Wouldn't that have been the final irony, if he'd succeeded in blowing himself up!"

"You should have made him hold the case," Marianna said.

"And carry it into the police station."

They were full of wild, silly bravado now that it was over. Boyd Currier listened somberly. He was shorter and heavier than Paul and a little broader through the face, but there was a strong family resemblance reinforced by their now almost identical haircuts. He turned to Marianna with concern. "They might at least have let you out of the car."

"I don't think it occurred to anyone—the idea of opening and closing a door, any jarring. Anyway, I don't think I'd have gone, not alone. In the state I was in, to be all by myself on the streets of Belgrade, no . . . I'd had enough. I would have stayed with Paul anyway, no matter what," she finished decisively.

"God, after everything I'd let you in for," Paul marveled. He would have moved toward her, she thought, but that would wait. A world of private explanations would have to come later.

Boyd was waiting, rather like a judge, trying to piece together the facts. "This Georgy," he prompted, taking what Marianna felt was a brotherly poke. "How in hell did he rope you in in the first place?"

Paul grimaced. "My sheltered life. I guess I've been away from government too long. I was losing my suspicious nature. It so happens," he went on as Boyd restrained a smile, "I'd worked with Georgy. Years ago he was one of our agents."

"You said you were with State," Marianna murmured.

"One said things like that." Paul shrugged. "Ostensibly I was. What I didn't realize was that Georgy had changed jobs, too—or had been moonlighting all along, playing at double agent. The first time I saw him—remember, Mari, on the boat coming into Hvar, you asked me who he was?"

She remembered very well: Paul had been annoyed.

"I thought I recognized him," he went on now. "I was pretty sure he was one of our boys, but he was evasive. He didn't want to talk to me right then, or be seen with me. I'm sure he didn't want you to see us together. They must have been working out their little scheme then, and Georgy wanted to know exactly where to find me—at any given time. He was lurking around that night, too. The night I charged out . . . like a damned fool," he added softly.

"If you'd only told me . . ."

"I know. I repeat, I was a damned fool. But I thought Georgy was my problem, I could handle him. You'd had enough of your own. If I'd had any idea . . ." He stopped as if overwhelmed by regret, and for a long moment they looked at each other without speaking. So much might have been so different.

Boyd cleared his throat. "As you were saying . . . this fellow Georgy's had his eye on you for some time apparently."

"I've wondered where they picked up my trail. In Split, I guess, when I first landed. And you"—he smiled at Marianna—"must have worried them. You were certainly an unexpected complication. No one else would have missed me. But then you gave them a hold over me, too. Once they had you, I wasn't about to do anything rash like tell them to go to hell. They could count on that. I can see Lotte's fine hand in there, sizing up that situation."

His direct look shut out Boyd for a moment. Marianna smiled, feeling warm suddenly and contented. "I'm glad *they* were so sure how you felt. I certainly wasn't when you took off, the way you just disappeared without a word."

"God." Paul clutched at his hair in helpless anger. "Mari, you've got to understand. You do understand now, don't you? I'd have given anything to get back and explain, but . . ."

"But?" she repeated softly.

"I'd better start at the beginning, when Georgy walked into that little café in Stari Grad. He didn't walk in exactly, he popped up outside the wall like some grade-B spook. You know. Psst." Paul crooked a beckoning finger and jerked his chin, leering like a dirty picture vendor.

"Strictly hush-hush. Didn't want the proprietor to see him. I went along with the gag. I thought I'd be back by the time you came out of the washroom. But then it got less funny."

Paul paused to sort out his thoughts. "Remember, I thought he was one of ours. He sounded well briefed, plausible enough. When he said the Agency had got wind of some dirty tricks involving the new ambassador, well, I'd half expected something of the sort."

"Is that why you came?" Boyd said, leaning forward, frowning.

"To keep an eye on big brother? Not really, but at this point in time"—Paul grinned—"it's not hard to imagine someone trying to make trouble between Yugoslavia and the U.S. We've been on pretty good terms for some time and developed some strong economic ties, as you well know—and so does Moscow, and it makes them nervous."

Boyd nodded and Marianna said, "Jack Dance said something about that. He was talking about how the Yugoslavs balance their relations between the Americans and the Russians and haven't aligned themselves with either side. And how the assassination of the American Ambassador could throw off the balance."

"To put it mildly," Boyd agreed.

"It made a convincing story anyway—not bad considering how fast they must have had to improvise. An effective smoke screen at least, at the time. We know now of course that Georgy's gang had much more ambitious plans, much bigger game in mind, with all due respect." Paul bowed to his brother. "But Georgy's story had me going: the idea that you were to be picked off en route to a ceremonial visit to the Presidential Palace—for maximum impact, symbolism, whatever; he put in some nice touches. I swallowed them anyway.

"And remember, he was hustling me away from the café as he told me all this, and whispering, making a big production of urgency and secrecy. It was just the sort of fool stunt the Agency would pull. That was my first reaction, while he was rushing me along and filling in details.

"What he was saying was that I had to be a sort of stalking horse—anyway, draw some unspecified assassin's attention away from you. If I understood Georgy, you had requested my help."

"I knew nothing about it, any of this," Boyd protested.

"No, of course not. I realize that now . . . and I should have then. I should have been a lot more suspicious. Maybe I would have been under different circumstances, but I was on vacation, and I'd just met Marianna. All your fault," he put in with the gentlest of smiles. "I just wanted to get back to that café before you wondered what in hell had happened.

"So there I was, trotting along with Georgy around the corner and out of sight, down along the dock to meet some other character. On a boat yet, where we wouldn't be seen conferring and couldn't possibly be overheard. As I said, it was as authentically crackpot as any Agency operation. Their idea was that I would pose as Ambassador—briefly, they assured me. Just on the crucial drive to the Palace, with Georgy next to me playing chargé d'affaires and the other operative as driver. Then behind, in an ordinary car, would be the rest of our team all ready to pounce on the mythical would-be assassin. With him rounded up, you would proceed safely on schedule and no one the wiser, no waves made or unpleasantness, all very diplomatic."

"It's insane, your risking your life as my stand-in."

"I couldn't agree more," said Paul cheerfully. "Exactly what I told them, but they weren't listening. Or

172

couldn't hear me with the engines racing. The bastards had the boat going full speed down the inlet. I'd been shanghaied! Me!"

Paul shook his head, disbelieving still. "Christ. I've never felt so stupid . . . or helpless. And mad! I could have killed them. Eventually, when I calmed down, they assured me that my girl would be taken care of, not to worry. They even apologized for handling things that way, but . . ."

"Taken care of," Marianna repeated bitterly. "I was taken care of all right, too well."

"They told the truth for once, then," Paul said with a certain grimness about the mouth. "The rest, of course, was all lies, pure fiction, an elaborate cover story for my benefit. They planned to pass me off as the American Ambassador for reasons that had nothing to do with Boyd's safety, as you well know. With a neat little bomb tucked into my papers. God, what a near thing. Can you imagine . . . the mayhem . . . if I'd succeeded in blowing up the Predsednik. To say nothing of myself."

"We would all have been blasted right out of the country," Boyd said. "There'd have been no hope of salvaging anything. Of *apologizing.*" He made a bitter joke of the word.

"If you hadn't got there, Mari, when you did . . ." Paul stopped as if overwhelmed by the alternatives. He looked closely at Marianna, then slid off the desk to stand next to her. "Are you all right?"

She felt bloodless, drained. Now that it was over, now

that Paul was here in front of her—and had not blown himself up, nor the Predsednik, nor U.S.-Yugoslavian friendship—she was suddenly speechless. It had been too near a miss. There had been too many times when she might have given up, when something might have gone differently, changing everything.

"It might," Boyd expressed her thought, "have been a real disaster. And I had no idea." It was his turn to be awed. "I had no idea what you two were going through. Everything seemed normal enough when I left the residence this morning. My briefcase, my papers . . ."

"Mine were forged, of course," said Paul. "Georgy had had a good deal of experience at that sort of thing. It was useful, when he worked for us."

"But you were late," Marianna remembered. She spoke slowly, puzzling this out. "You must have been, or I never would have made it in time."

"I was slightly delayed, yes. First by a crackpot call about a bomb, some hysterical woman." Boyd's smile was penitent. "We get a lot of those. We check them out, of course, but there was obviously nothing wrong. The real problem was that detour. Road repairs, I assumed at the time—there was some sort of barricade and a colossal traffic jam. I'm afraid I wasn't paying much attention. My chauffeur is perfectly competent and I was in the back, thinking about my interview with the Predsednik. We were finally directed onto some roundabout route and in the process apparently picked up a nail or something that cut the tire. Anyway, it went flat and had to be changed."

"Resourceful bastards," said Paul. "They certainly weren't taking any chances on your catching up with me. Meanwhile, there I was, steaming along in your place, expecting to be waylaid. You must have begun to wonder about the delays, one damned thing after another."

"I felt a little jinxed, I'll admit. And I was getting nervous about being late. It's considered very bad form on these occasions, gets one off on the wrong foot altogether. I needed a highly diplomatic excuse. It seemed tactless to blame the streets of the capital."

"So what did you blame?"

"American automotive genius. I said we'd had car trouble. The Predsednik was delighted."

Paul laughed. "The height of diplomacy. There's nothing more tactful than knocking good old American know-how. Hey, speaking of saving face, mine is feeling slightly underfed."

"Good Lord, lunch! What would you like?"

"A bath to start," Marianna said. "And clean clothes and a comb."

"With a double martini on the side," Paul added.

"And all the fixings," they finished in ragged harmony as Boyd rang for his secretary.

"But what about Ivo?" Marianna asked.

"I wouldn't worry. He'll be along, I'm sure, though they may not want to release him right away. It may take time. To pin all those medals on him," Boyd explained hastily, "now that he's a national hero."

Chapter 18

It was too strange, the idea of going back, perhaps not possible, Marianna felt.

"Like replaying a nightmare backwards," she said uncertainly on the plane, trying to make Paul understand her dragging reluctance.

"All the more reason why you should. You've got to," he said, his hand closing over hers on the armrest between their seats. "You can't keep running away, darling. You've got to exorcise your ghosts." He smiled his apology. He had been taking this rather excessively positive attitude for some time, jollying her. "And I want to see this monastery of yours."

She shivered. "Not mine."

"It doesn't sound quite real. Another Brigadoon. Anyway, you want your own clothes back, don't you? And there's the slight problem of your passport."

"And the slight problem of Jack Dance's death."

He was startled by her bitterness. "Damn Jack Dance. Good riddance. If he's the one we think he is . . . was . . . you should get a medal."

"No. Please. Don't even say it. If I killed him, too . . ."

"Sorry." Paul was quiet for a moment, scowling with concern, then burst out: "But Dance was a bastard. Literally, in fact. Danza was his real name, according to our records. We've got quite a dossier on him. He was the son of an Italian girl and an American G.I. who went home to his wife at the end of World War Two. Danza grew up bitter, badly warped by hatred for the father who'd deserted him and I gather spent his life trying to get even with the whole U.S.A. He started out as a Communist in Italy, tried to get to the States but couldn't get a visa, so he got mixed up with a particularly nasty terrorist group, rabidly pro-Soviet, whose chief mission seems to have been handing Yugoslavia over to the Russians. This would suit Danza to a tee, anything to hurt the U.S. Don't give that punk a thought. He wouldn't have had any qualms about killing you. One word from Georgy and . . ."

She turned her head away, shutting out what he was saying, and rested her forehead against the vibrating window. The lovely soft plain of the Danube was falling away below them. Ahead were the stony, spiky mountains, gray and forbidding as the surface of the moon.

"Look, Mari, there's nothing to worry about," Paul said after a time. He would have put his arm around her —he reached out once, but apparently found the position too awkward or her tightly angled back unreceptive. "They're not likely to prosecute, anything like that. They won't blame you . . . in the circumstances," he finished vaguely.

She was trying to remember how it had been exactly, the thrashing black water and the feel of the knife in her hand, sinking into something, she had thought. "I didn't mean to kill him." She spoke in a flat murmur and Paul leaned close to hear. "I didn't mean to kill Ted either."

"It wasn't your fault. You can't take the blame for either one of them."

"No? Maybe not. But they're both dead. I was there, and I can't help feeling . . . Paul"—she turned to him suddenly—"do you think I'm a Jonah?"

His smile widened gradually. "Typhoid Mary maybe. It's the chance I'll have to take. Glad to."

"Seriously . . ."

"Seriously." But he was laughing.

There was a great deal more that they might have said if Ivo's head had not appeared at that moment, rising over the back of the next seat like an auspicious planet. Sensing what he had interrupted, he grinned, and Marianna found herself grinning back at him, like an idiot, with tears streaming down her cheeks.

It was Ivo who took over then—all the decisions and arrangements were his—rather as if people in love were known incompetents. He had not been a tour guide for nothing, he reminded them grandly—juggling timetables, selecting routes and cars and boats—

and would continue to be one as long as heroism was not a paying proposition.

"We could never have got here without you," Paul conceded in the final stage of their approach to Melita. The white sunstruck shape of the monastery was just emerging from the green frame of its island, not quite real yet. Paul studied it in silence, impressed.

"You swam this?"

"Over there. Then we walked." Marianna traced the long curve of their rocky path and, remembering the stumbling darkness, found it, too, unreal. She had been wet, freezing, nearly naked until Nico gave her his shirt.

"There is a legend," Ivo began in his best tour guide manner, "that Saint Paul was shipwrecked here on his way to Rome . . ."

Paul smiled and pulled Marianna close.

"In the thirteenth century an order of Benedictine monks . . ." Ivo went on, unheard.

"Jack Dance said you'd come here," Marianna murmured into Paul's shoulder. She closed her eyes, giving herself up to the luxury of his closeness. "You've made an honest man of him." She could feel his cheek move when he smiled.

"The best lies," he said, "have a kernel of truth."

"Umm." She did not open her eyes again until the engines were cut and they were gliding toward the stone landing. With a flourish Ivo tossed the line to someone and jumped ashore.

Marianna gasped. There was no mistaking the tall,

long-armed figure who secured the line. But this was not the shambling, smoldering Nico. The boat tied, he straightened up with a look of pride and offered Marianna a gallant hand.

"So what happened? I still don't understand," Marianna said.

For ceremonial purposes they had gathered around a tiny subterranean bar, and Nico was dispensing *šljivovica* with proprietary abandon. This part of the monastery was new to her, as was the whole cordial atmosphere, the evidence that this was in fact a hotel, now filling with holiday business. In the arched dining room a long row of tables had been set for dinner.

They raised their glasses to each other, the four of them, and Paul proposed a toast, "To heroes!"—which Nico did not understand but drank to agreeably.

For some time Marianna had been feeling left out while Paul and Ivo—interrupting each other and stumbling over an assortment of language barriers—questioned Nico. In their eagerness to get at the facts, they had neglected to share them. "Tell me!" she ordered Ivo this time.

"He says that the man . . ."

"Danza," Paul supplied. "Your Jack Dance."

". . . did not die of knife wounds," Ivo persisted. "He was"—circling his throat graphically with his hands—"strangled."

"Friend Nico here," Paul interjected, "knew that all

along, having done it himself." At the mention of his name Nico beamed and nodded.

"But he wouldn't admit it. At the time," Marianna said, "he blamed me. He told the police that I'd killed Jack Dance."

Paul smiled. "He didn't know then what a popular move it was going to be. When it turned out that Danza's death was a good thing—anyone who'd endanger the Predsednik—he was glad to confess, to take the credit. He's become something of a hero, too. We're surrounded by heroes." He extended his glass for a refill.

"I see," Marianna said, slowly fitting the pieces together. "I only wish he'd acted a little sooner. I don't know why he didn't, the way Jack goaded him."

"But he was afraid," Ivo put in quickly, "for the monastery. He did not want it destroyed, this beautiful place. But then, when you tried to escape and this terrible man went after you . . ." Ivo paused, teasing.

"He rushed to my rescue!" Marianna said. "I don't believe it."

"No. Maybe not. The truth is," Ivo admitted, "when I asked him what happened, he could not explain. He went crazy is all he could say."

A good kind of crazy, Marianna thought, remembering his strange gruff kindness. His shirt. She would have liked to be able to talk to him but could only raise her glass in his direction and exchange tentative smiles.

181

"And what about Lotte?" she said then. "Don't tell me she deserves a medal, too."

Paul laughed and put the question to Nico, continuing to smile through Nico's shrugs and gestures. "It seems," he translated at last, "that the lady did not wait for Nico's return. He assumes that she got one look at Jack Dance's body and lit out of here. By rowboat. He found it on the other side."

The image of Lotte rowing away, her rings sparkling on the oars, was lovely. "I'm sure she made it," Marianna said. "People like Lotte always seem to land on their feet."

"Or their backs," Paul murmured.

Marianna smiled and sipped her drink. "That's nice," she said, "when you think about it. Neat. Ivo gets a medal for snatching the bomb out of your hands. Nico gets credit for removing Jack Dance. Lotte gets away . . ."

"And you," said Paul without hesitation, "get me."

"I see," she said again. There seemed to be no decision involved. No problem, in any case.